GETTING HERE

STORIES SELECTED BY RUDY WIEBE

NeWest Press

ISBN 0-920316-00-X

NeWest Press
13024-109 Avenue
Edmonton, Alberta, Canada
T5M 3N3

How did you get here? I asked.

The question's not how I got here, but why I came, he said. When I heard you were coming, I couldn't resist coming too. I keep my ear to the ground, he said.

Sheila Watson, *The Black Farm*

For permission to reprint copyright material grateful acknowledgement is made to the following:

Sheila Watson and The Macmillan Company of Canada for permission to quote from " The Black Farm " originally published in *Queen's Quarterly* , Summer, 1956 and reprinted in *Stories From Western Canada* selected by Rudy Wiebe and published by The Macmillan Company of Canada.

Cover photo by Harvey Spak

CONTENTS

A WOMAN OF MODERATE TEMPERAMENT

Aritha van Herk

When he wasn't around, she couldn't remember what her husband looked like. It was as if she needed his presence to be sure that he was real. Drying her hands on the striped linen dishtowel, she went into the living room and stared at his graduation portrait on the buffet. An unsmiling pose, but he became immediately real, almost present in the large, openspaced room. She stood in front of the framed photograph a long time, trying to assimilate the contours of his face. But when she turned away he vanished again; there was nothing but a residue of his belongings in the room: the pipe on the magazine table, the brown sweater flung over the back of the chair. She had to force herself not to stand staring at the glossy photograph inside the gilt frame. In the kitchen again, she tried drawing his picture in her mind, but the faintly derisive face that appeared was that of a stranger, a face outlined with black charcoal.

They were all of a kind in the night class. Fugitive students, taking courses for pleasure or necessity but none of them professional, making a career of learning. She knew the rest were like her, with houses and spouses and perhaps children or impending children. It was the professor's good deed: two hours a week for the outside world, for housewives and businessmen. The woman on her right in a pantsuit and well-manicured hair; the man on her left in a blue shirt and striped tie. Week after week.

" I've had a very interesting life, " he said. " We should have coffee some time and I could tell you my life story. It's fascinating. "

She didn't quite know what to say to the familiar stranger's first words and his obvious intention. She smiled politely. " Sure. "

" No, really, " he persisted. " It's very interesting. "

" That's what everyone says. " She refused to grapple with his insistence.

" You don't believe me, do you? Well, let me tell you, I've travelled all over the world, I'm a lawyer. You look like an intelligent person; you'd enjoy my stories. "

" You're presuming. "

" Why are you taking a night course then? "

She didn't want to commit herself and shrugged. " Just for something to do. "

" Do you work? "

She hesitated, finally shook her head.

" Are you married? "

" I don't see why that should concern you."

" Come on, it's just an ordinary question."

She stared at him. " Maybe we've been sitting beside each other in this class for the last four weeks, but you are really pushy."

" Sorry," he said, " but you're attractive and I'm just interested."

She turned to the front of the brightly-lit room where the professor was opening a book on the lectern, studiously ignoring him and trying not to betray the tension she felt beside him.

Why were these rooms always so brightly-lit? It was as if the students were plants forced to grow despite their desire for darkness and rest. The tables at which they sat were metal with coated and polished wooden tops. Everything so artificial: the light, the furniture, even the professor, arms gesturing like a silent movie.

After class he turned to her again, shutting his notebook deliberately. " Well, are you married? "

She stared at him. " Are you? "

" Yes. And I've got four kids." He grinned and turned to go. " See you next week."

At night she grappled with him, the strength of his arms and legs trapping her. His smile when she closed the bedroom door.

" Turn off the light."

" I want it on," she said.

" What for? Turn it off."

" I want to look at you, I want to be able to watch you." She was almost pleading.

" It hurts my eyes," he said, rolling on his side. " Turn it off."

The white curtains billowed from the open win-

The white curtains billowed from the open window in the almost darkness. His arm slid around her under the covers, touched her hair. " How's my wife? "

" I'm fine," she said. And felt him, the same warm and muscled strength.

" Are you tired? "

" Just a little," her voice seemed disembodied in the shadowed room.

His hands were a brush of warmth down her backbone, down her legs, across her breasts. He was familiar, familiar, silent yet quick-breathing, as familiar as her own hands. But his face was in shadow above her and his features were strange; she wanted to see his eyes, grey-blue, to know it was really him — really him and not a stranger: even his breathing not enough.

She lay awake beside him in the dark while he slept.

"How are you tonight? " He had a slight accent, a remnant of some country she could not place.

"Not too great." She was determined to be disagreeable.

"Oh, why not?"

"I don't know, just not too great."

"I don't know your name," he said. "I'm Lev Rosen."

"Miriam Kenner," she said shortly.

"Miriam, that's a Jewish name."

"No, it's not. I had a romantic mother."

"I'm Jewish. It's one of the interesting things about me."

"Oh really. Does it make you that special?" She wanted to be sarcastic, to inflict on him what grated her.

" Of course, it's all a part of it. I've travelled all over the world; I just came to Canada four years ago from Poland; I've had a very interesting life."

" You told me that before."

" It's true, it's true. I've got my own business, a wife, four children, a mistress—."

"You admit having a mistress."

" Why not? It's a part of my life. If you gave me a chance, I could tell you a lot more."

" Usually people who say they've had an interesting life haven't at all."

" Well, I have—how old are you?"

"Twenty-three."

"God, I wish I was your age. Between twenty and thirty is the best time of your life. You can do anything. If you want to make a lot of money, if you want to travel, if you want to screw your heart out. What do you do?"

She hesitated. " I just take some courses."

"How many?"

"Three, I'm finishing up my degree."

"Well, I'm taking three courses; I'm running a business, and I work as a lawyer full time."

"So, what is that supposed to prove?"

"Nothing, just that I'm really busy, and I wish I was younger so I could do more."

She watched him furtively during the class: a disagreeable little man, a squashed, pudgy, greasy little man with quick dark eyes. She could taste her revulsion but there was something in his eyes that held her attention, an unnamable attraction.

She could feel the locket swinging against her

breastbone. When she wore it she was always consciously aware of the hinged, flat compartment gleaming silver against her throat. Its engraved weight on the delicate chain almost a musical clash against her skin, the coldness of the silver producing a vibration in her nerves. Always aware of it and him, a miniature representation revealed when the tiny hinges clicked open. The sheltering oval within the locket was like a reavowal or a reminder of an initiation rite.

Looking from the small silver frame, his face was defiant, unsmiling, jaw thrust out. She could sense that his arms were folded, his backbone stiff. For the camera? For the person with the camera? The eyes were as steady and abrasive as grains of sand.

She wore it periodically, sometimes for days at a time without taking it off. It harassed her neck while she slept so that in the mornings she woke with faint marks on her skin from the chain. Sometimes, she didn't wear it for weeks, then put it on, hands fumbling with the tiny clasp. Surprised to feel its weight and its splashing movement against her skin, vulnerable and receptive after being so long unencumbered. He toyed with it when she wore it, but didn't notice its absence. It was his gift but her whim, her desire.

Wearing the chain, she felt his fingers: their smooth path down the middle of her back, the pressure of her bones tensing under his touch as brittle as a bird's beneath the weight of his light, dry palm. That cool, demanding caress brought her involuntary response every time, made her turn full towards him and move to extinguish their individual shadows, to rout the silence of the darkness.

" You got time for coffee?"

" I guess I have, a few minutes." She wanted to retract it the minute she agreed.

Seated across the table from him, she felt again that sense of revulsion. His round face and double chin gave him a look of well-fed oiliness, and suddenly shivering, she saw in his quick dark eyes some resemblance to an inquisitive rat.

He stared at her while she traced patterns on the table with her finger, played with the packets of sugar.

"What does your husband do?"

She raised her eyes from his hands; he wore nothing on them.

"He's a...," she hesitated. " Why? "

"I'm interested." He watched her calmly.

" He's just an ordinary man."

He snorted. " We're all more or less ordinary. What does he do?"

" Does it matter?"

" Of course not. Only I'm curious."

" He's a chartered accountant."

" That's interesting. And you just go to school?"

" You've asked me that before," she said defensively.

" Well, I'm interested." He spread his hands. "Obviously you don't have to work if your husband is a chartered accountant. But what do you enjoy? What do you intend to do?"

" Right now I just want to finish my degree."

" In what?"

" Psychology."

" And then what?"

She resented the question, but felt forced to justify herself. " I'm not sure. Maybe I can get a job in the school system or something. I'd like to work with children."

" Do you have any children?"

" No," she said quickly, " no ."

" How long have you been married?"

" About four years." She stopped abruptly. "Why are you asking me all these questions?"

" Why are you answering them?"

" I don't know. I don't usually answer personal questions," she said angrily.

" Don't get mad." He smiled at her. " I make it my business to interrogate people — I'm a lawyer, you know."

" I know," she said. " You told me."

" Well, are you happy in your marriage? If you had some kids, you could practice your psychology on your own kids."

" No thanks."

" I'm married," he said. " I've got kids, four of them. I just find it hard to keep up with everything, what with my family and my two businesses."

" You run two businesses?" She was relieved to turn the conversation to him.

"Yes, I'm a lawyer and I'm also in the importing business."

She played idly with the handle of her cup. " Oh, what do you import?"

" Wine. Some jewellery. Mostly precious stones."

"From where? "

" Amsterdam — it's the diamond distribution centre of the world."

" Diamonds?" she said lazily. " Isn't that illegal?"

" No , it's not illegal at all. It's necessary to get

a permit and to pay duty, but there's nothing illegal about it and it's a good business.

She looked at her watch furtively, wondering when she could make a polite excuse to leave. But she made an effort. " Well, that is fascinating, importing diamonds."

" Mostly diamonds," he said matter-of-factly. " A few emeralds and rubies."

Inexplicably, the words in his mouth shocked her. She had only associated gems with turbaned princes in eastern palaces, and she suddenly realized she had never thought of rubies and emeralds in contemporary life at all, and certainly not in connection with such ratty little men. They belonged only to the past or to royalty, casual and commonplace playthings of people so far removed that to her they were mystical, mythological and non-existent in the regular world. She drew a deep breath.

" Don't look so surprised," he said. " It's a perfectly ordinary thing to do."

" I don't believe you," she said. "You're telling me a big story."

" No, I'm not."

" Besides, I'm sure it's illegal."

" Look, it's not illegal at all. I've even been investigated by the RCMP because someone as naive as you told them I was doing something illegal. My papers are impeccable; I'm perfectly clear and above-board." He laughed. " You don't believe me, well, sometime when I've just got a shipment, I'll bring some to show to you. I should be getting one soon."

" How do you get them? With an armoured car? "

" In the mail."

She shook her head. " In the mail how?"

" In a little box in the regular mail."

" You're crazy."

" No, it's perfectly safe."

She shook her head again, almost bewildered. " It still sounds crazy. Then what do you do with them?"

" I sell them."

" Do you make a lot of money?"

" Well, enough. There's not much of a market for luxuries like jewels in Canada. People here don't appreciate their value as unusual pieces. That's why I import mostly diamonds. I usually sell them for twice what I pay and the jewellery stores usually sell them for twice what they pay me."

" That's robbery."

" I have to live. I have a wife and family, an expensive new house and furniture and a mistress to keep."

" Why do you keep bringing up your mistress?"

He laughed shortly. " Sorry. Maybe it's because I'm afraid of getting old. That's one reason why I take night classes; it keeps me up to date on what's happening."

She looked at him, and he laughed again. " I'm thirty-six. Thirty-six! How old are you?"

" Twenty-three."

" God, if I was twenty-three again. Between twenty and thirty, those are the best years of anyone's life. You can do anything you want — to extremes. Those were the years when I travelled all through Europe, when I did my most successful work, when I could do anything. And you don't even appreciate it."

She put the laundry basket full of clean towels down and went into the bedroom. Her husband didn't like his high school picture in the living room because everyone noticed it and commented on it. " Oh is that you? You look so different now. You were such a nice-looking boy." The features of the squarish face were familiar, but she could not connect the youthfulness of the picture to the way he was now — his features did not have that same soft, blind sheen, the totally closed and unaware perfection of the slight and imperfect schoolboy face.

In the dim bedroom at night, his profile on the other pillow was familiar but vague, more like memory than reality. She wanted to wake him and say, " Tell me a real secret about yourself, something I don't know, something that would really show me something about you." She watched him asleep, always lying on his back, relaxed but composed, a blind face sculpted in soft, warm stone. Lying close but not touching him, she watched, waited for him to reveal something, eventually fell asleep watching, waiting.

" Hey," he said. " Let's go for coffee. I've got something to show you."

" Alright." Her agreement seemed to set her teetering on an edge, but she could not refuse, had not the power. " What is it?"

" Well, you didn't believe me, did you?"

She forced a laugh. " I won't believe it until I see it."

At the small table, he took the envelope from his pocket and unfolded the white tissue from inside it. "There," he said.

They lay like fragments of broken colour, unaware of their immutable perfection, gleaming iridescent like rich fruit in the light. She felt her face naked, looking at them and their faceted refractions.

He watched her, eyes steady and calculating. "They are beautiful, aren't they," he said quietly.

She could not raise her eyes. " They are," she said, hushed. Suddenly accusing, " How can you dare to carry them around like that?"

" What better way is there? Do you think I should carry around a safety deposit box?"

" I guess it would be ridiculous." She put out a finger, then drew back. " Can I touch them?"

" Yes, just be careful, I know how many there are." Then quickly, " I'm only joking."

She scarcely heard him. Turning them gently with the tip of her finger they seemed to glow against her short, unpolished nail with a milky rosiness. They could have been splinters of glass, but everything echoed their coloured reflections; the dull surface of the bare formica table was illuminated. The torn and grubby university cafe became clean and crystalline under their refracted light. And suddenly, in them she saw a memory of what she longed for: the movement in life that she was seeking and had never been close to.

" Are they terribly expensive?"

" Over a thousand dollars each," he said.

" I wish I could buy one." She laughed. " That's silly. They're for rich people."

" Surely your husband can afford to buy you one."

The idea shocked her. " Oh no, it's ridiculous to buy something so extravagant."

" Well, if you ever want to get one, it's cheaper

buying from me than a jeweller. Keep it in mind. And if you ever need anything, just let me know. I can get you just about anything you want."

In the shower, she tipped her head back under the hot cascade. It struck her skin with the force of a million tiny stones: an enormous vitality pouring over her and relieving her tension. She offered her body to the water with gratitude, gradually relaxing into its force and heat until she became a part of its fluidity, its incomprehensible sheen. Inside that vortex was a completeness in itself, composed only of the jewelled liquid and her body, the two merging to a single refraction of light. She thought of a spectator watching her moving under the flow of water, skin slick and wet, shining like a polished surface, hair misted with diamonds, streams of water cascading down the emerald curves of her skin. She moved for him, the audience, the voyeur, turning and glistening to show her well-cut lines. She enjoyed herself, liked herself as nowhere else, her breasts, her back, her legs long and smooth and beyond themselves. Polished the water over her skin, accepted its force and herself nothing more than a beautiful particle in the vortex. Saw them all watching, the shower curtain vanished, herself stepping in ballet under the water, admired but unreachable.

In the sunlight through the bright curtains, she thought of the dim light in the bedroom at night, the gleaming locket lying on the dresser, waiting to be worn. She lay with her back to him staring at the bare wall, the empty spaces of paint. Thought of her husband.

Even with an undefinable face, the tension of his body, the smooth muscular quality of his presence, his inscrutable but passionate face. And that hard, definitive touch, that powerful gentleness that she had not known before.

His hand on her back was sweaty, not a warm, smooth sweep but a hot, random journey. She lay still, refusing to turn around; refusing everything. But the refusal now was nothing compared to the acceptance she had made, nothing at all.

HUNTING SEASON

Helen J. Rosta

She saw the footprints early one morning, directly below her cabin in the soft muck around the beaver dam, first one, and then a few yards further on, another. She followed them until they disappeared on the hard ground that led into the trees. Then she turned back, and straddling one of the prints, stood for a long time looking at it. It was sunk deeply into the mud, a large oval heel and five toes, the big toe nearly the size of her hand, as if, during the night, a giant had walked across the field. She wondered what they had used to make it.

She heard the putt-putt of his truck and looked up just as it was rising over the brow of the hill. For a moment she thought of moving into the shadow of trees and waiting... She could imagine him with his ear close to the cabin door listening ot the sound of his knocking reverberate through the two rooms, and when he was satisfied that she wasn't there, turning away, his hand shading his eyes, slowly scanning the countryside for a a sight of her... then sauntering, heavy-footed, to the corral where Star would whinny to him, stopping to pet her, whistling softly through his gap teeth... continuing on to the barn, peering into the stalls, climbing the stars to the hayloft... down again ... and over to the garage, which was locked, and windowless...

He got out of the truck. She could hear the tinny sound as the door slammed shut. When his back was toward her, she started away from the trees at a dead run, circling the hill so that when he saw her he wouldn't know where she had come from. He was still pounding on the door when she walked up behind him.

"There's nobody in there," she said.

He turned and a smile spread over his long, sun-reddened face. " Some people are up and about early."

The cabin was warm inside. She stirred the fire and set the coffee pot on the stove. He pulled up a chair to the table, took off his red hunter's cap, placed it on his knee and clasped his hands around it. His hands were large and square the fingernails flat and rimmed with grease.

" When hunting season starts you shouldn't wander around without something red on, " he told her.

" My land's posted," she said.

" They don't always pay attention to that... there's lots of game hiding out in this bush."

" But it is my land..."

" Doesn't matter whose land it is ...during hunting season you wear something red." He smiled, showing big, gap teeth and then covered his mouth with his hand, speaking from behind it. " They say this year maybe they'll bag the old maid over on the Coulter place."

" It's not the Coulter place anymore," she said and then added, " Nobody's going to bag anything on my land."

" Now don't go getting mad. You know how people talk." He took his hand away from his mouth.

" I just don't want them tramping all over the place..." She thought of the tracks down by the beaver pond and for a moment considered taking him down and showing them to him but then the image of the hand covering his smile came to her... probably he knew about the footprints already, had helped plot them, and was waiting for her to say something so that he could go back and tell his buddies.. Maybe he had been one of them, skulking about her place in the dead of night.

" I came to help you trim the mare's feet," he said.

" But you've been here nearly everyday doing something for me." Everyday, she thought, everyday... and he's the only one. " I can do them."

" I came to help," he said. He stood up. smoothed his hair and set the red cap on his head.

She led the way out to the corral. " You're doing too much for me, " she continued, " I appreciate it, but you have your own work..." He whistled and Star whirled about, ran toward them, and then stood stockstill, ears pricked, watching their approach.

" Trimmers still in the barn? " He started toward it. He knows where everything is, she thought. She climbed over the railing into the corral and put an arm around the mare's neck. She could feel a quiver moving like a ripple under the skin. He emerged from the barn, watched for a moment, then unfastened the gate and came into the corral, the hoof trimmers in one hand.

" You hang onto the halter," he said. " I'll take care of the feet." He ran his hand over the horse's neck and shoulder, bent down, slid his hand along the leg, straddled it, and grabbing the fetlock pulled the leg back toward him. The horse reared up, jerking the halter from her hand and knocking him to the ground. He swore, picked himself up, and lunged for the halter.

" Don't! " She grabbed his sleeve. "Leave it for now. She's trembling... something's frightened her." They did, she thought, prowling around.

" Shouldn't let her get away like that. She'll try it next time." He seemed undecided, standing, slightly stooped, the hoof trimmers still in his hand.

" She's too nervous."

" Shouldn't let her get away."

" Something's frightened her," she repeated. " Do you have any idea what it might have been? "

" Horses spook easy...maybe one of those wild animals you've been harbouring scared her."

She saw the beginnings of the smile, turned her back and walked ahead of him. " It *is* my land. I don't have to let them hunt it."

" They've always hunted this land." He paused and gazed toward the dark line of trees behind the beaver dam. " You know how they are."

" No," she said, " I don't know how they are. I never see any of them."

" They're kind of shy," he said, " that is the bachelors are shy, and the married ones..." The hand went over his mouth. " Course being a widower, none of that applies to me..." He looked away, letting the words hang in the air. " And the women...people don't like what they don't understand."

" What don't they understand?"

" They wonder what's a woman doing out here all alone."

" I've got as much right to be here as anyone."

" Oh, it isn't a question of right. They wonder, that's all."

" How do they feel about you coming here?"

" Oh, I get teased but I can take a joke."

" I imagine," she said, " that everyone around here really loves... a good joke."

He waved his hand toward the craggy, sombre hills covered with dense clumps of trees. " To survive in this country, you've got to have a sense of humour."

After he left, she rushed down to the beaver dam and inspected the tracks, again following them to where they disappeared, pausing on the margin of the trees, peering into the shadows, listening, turning back... They must have gone to a lot of trouble to make the footprints, she thought, and how could they be sure she'd even find them... unless they were watching her... knew her habits, the walk by the beaver dam in the early mornings, the rides along the fencelines.

Two days later she found her mailbox, still attached to its post, lying in the ditch beside the road. The side with her name on it was shoved in, the lid ajar. She dragged the box up to the roadbed, reached inside and felt for the letter which she had placed there the previous evening. She found the envelope. It was covered with black smudges and one end had been slit. The letter was gone. She held the envelope gingerly by one corner and studied it. They've left fingerprints, she thought. She was standing beside the road, the envelope still in her hand when he drove up. He stopped the truck beside her, jumped out, and started to throw tools from the back.

" Aren't you lucky," he said, " that I've been carting around all this fencing stuff."

She didn't move. " How did you know it was torn down? "

" Didn't. Just happened to be going by and saw you standing here. Like I said, you're lucky." He got a hammer from his tool kit and started to tap out the side of the box. " Guess you'll have to do without mail today."

" If I had any, the mailman could have brought it to me."

" Maybe when he saw the box gone, he figured that you didn't want any." He gave the box a final tap with the hammer, stood up and rubbed his hands on his trousers. " Good as new. Now all we have to do is dig another hole and set it up again." He picked up the post-hole auger, leaned his weight on it, and began to move rhythmically in a circular motion.

" This time they've gone too far." She shoved the envelope under his nose. " They've stolen my letter and that's a criminal offence."

" I wouldn't go making a fuss about it... it's nothing serious."

" Serious! They could go to jail for this." She waved the envelope at him. " Fingerprints all over. Look at it."

He snatched the envelope from her, wadded it up and stuffed it in his pocket. " When I get the box up, you can send another letter easy enough." He lifted the auger out of the hole and emptied the dirt from it. " Ground's moist. It won't take any time at all to get that thing standing. " He set the auger back in the ground.

" They stole my letter! "

He gave a violent twist to the auger, stopped and looked straight at her. "Was there anything in that letter you wouldn't want people to see?"

She kicked the ground angrily. " It's nobody's business what's in my letters."

He reached into his pocket, extracted the envelope and smoothed it out on the auger handle. When he had finished examining it, he put it back in his pocket and smiled at her. " That looks like a business letter to me. I've been to Edmonton. Think I've been in that store."

" I was ordering a gun."

He started working again. " Any money in that letter?"

" No... but it's stealing anyway...it's a federal offence to tamper with the mail."

" A gun won't do you any good," he said.

" What do you mean?"

" Can't hunt on your own land if it's posted."

" I wasn't going to hunt."

" Then what do you want a gun for? "

" Target practice."

" You don't need practice to hit a target," he said, " as long as it isn't moving."

He set up the mailbox in silence. She helped him tamp dirt and gravel around its base and carry the tools back to the truck.

" They could go to jail," she said.

He started to load the tools into the truck as if he hadn't heard her. When he had finished, he said, " You know, maybe you should get yourself a gun after all." He paused and gazed in the direction of her cabin, " Seems like they've noticed some kind of funny tracks leading onto your land."

" What kind of tracks? "

" You noticed anything? "

" What kind of tracks? " she asked again.
He shrugged. " I don't know...funny tracks...
maybe you should take a look for them."

" Why are they doing this to me? "

" Nobody's doing anything to you." He gestured toward the mailbox. " That's nothing."

" They've done other things."

" A few jokes..."

" My letter was no joke."

He climbed into the truck, started the engine,
then rolled down the window and leaned out. " You
didn't thank me," he said.

" I'm thanking you,but as far as I'm concerned,
the rest of them should go to jail. "

He started to roll up the window and his words
drifted back to her over the roar of the engine, "Hunting season starts tomorrow."

That afternoon, she saddled Star and rode
around the fencelines. South of the beaver dam, she
found a dead tree lying across the wire. She dismounted,
tied the horse to a sapling and, thinking that they had
pushed the tree onto the fence, examined the ground
for footprints. She found none. She grasped the trunk
and tried to swing the tree off the wire. It moved slowly
in an arc, its limbs catching in the branches of the trees
surrounding it. She struggled with it, her breath coming
in short, quick gasps. Star snorted and pawed impatiently. Suddenly, the tree broke loose and crashed to the
ground. The mare reared back, nostrils flaring.

She approached the horse, speaking softly,
" Whoa Star... easy girl... take it easy." She ran her
hand along the quivering side. All at once, the mare be-

came rigid, head up, ears forward. She turned slowly, following the mare's gaze.

It didn't move, just stood, looking at her, its hairy body towering among the trees, hands resting at its sides, its eyes a pale translucent amber, large, luminous, and full of fear.

The horse, as if she'd finally caught an alien scent, snorted and plunged. The creature stepped back, turned, and with huge strides, vanished into the shadows like an apparition.

Early next morning, the shots started. The first one was faint, far to the north-east. The next was louder, and the next. By dawn, they were sounding in a steady, staccato rhythm, closer, closer, one after the other. By nightfall, she imagined that they had advanced to the borders of her property.

That evening when she heard his truck, she waited silently behind the closed curtains, listening to the sound of his fist on the door. After a time, she heard him move away from the door, around the cabin, in front of the window, pause, then on... She thought she heard Star whinny softly and the thin sound of whistling. Finally, she heard the truck door slam and the roar of his engine as he drove away.

She listened to the roar fading in the distance, then opened the door and peered out. The moon was high, a large silver disc in the black sky. Below the cabin, the beaver pond gleamed like a pale circle of light. Behind it, the trees lay in impenetrable darkness. She thought of the creature crouching among the trees, its long arms resting on its knees, hands motionless, eyes large and luminous as the moon, staring into darkness.

Shortly after midnight, she heard the trucks. The

trucks. The sound cut through the cold air like the thud of wings. She ran to the window and looked out. The trucks came slowly up the road, gleaming shapes, lights extinguished, moving like a caravan. One by one they stopped outside the cabin and the dark figures alighted. At first she thought he wasn't with them, but then she saw his truck, saw him step down.

He joined the others, and they all walked together, their long, black shadows moving ahead of them.

SHOWDOWN

Myrna Kostash

Her mum and dad told her to call him
Uncle Andy. " This is your Uncle Andy.
He went to high school with your daddy." And they lifted her up under the
arms and sat her down face-to-face on
Uncle Andy's knee. He bounced her up
and down and she giggled, enjoying
herself. He came often to the house,
bringing little presents which he wouldn't
let her take until she had given him
a kiss and a hug. When she was five, he
was her babysitter and one night when
she was sleeping, he put his arm under
the bedclothes, his hand under her
nightie and his finger into the soft,
fleshy lips of her sex. She woke up,
feeling like she was being drilled.

She was walking backwards on the soft shoulder of the highway, thumb stuck out. Whoosh, whoosh, and whoosh again. Ha, who said chicks never had trouble hitch-hiking? But she, of course, refused to be coquettish. Just look at her: baggy blue jeans, sloppy t-shirt, pendulous breasts swinging untidily beneath, dusty face and matted mop of a hair-do. Not exactly a driver's fantasy of crumpet. Whoosh. Jeez. High noon and it was hot, goddam it. She stopped, sat down on her knapsack and lit up a cigarette —Formula X — and enjoyed for a few moments the adrenalin rush of dope and pure hatred. Fuckin' bastards, petty bourgeois sons of bitches, anal-clenching property owners, look at those stunned and porky faces as they rush on down the road, as if I didn't pay taxes along with the rest of them. She had exchanged hitch-hiking tales with James and he had reported the same thing: it was the tourists who were the worst, their self-righteous faces and smug kids gawking out the windows at the freak show with the stuck-out thumbs, and it would take a local peasant with a donkey cart, for God's sake, to get him to the next watering hole.

James. Probably still in bed at noon, dead to the world, his body only half-covered by the sheet trailing off the side of the mattress. I could be there. He awakens slowly, leans over my sleeping body, gently pushes up the nylon swishiness of my naughty nightie (one soft, plush breast is peeking out the neckline) and lies down atop me and I awake very slowly, surfacing languidly into my flesh, feeling the soothing strokes of James' cock as he slides like a dancer inside my spaces, ah, that's lovely. She threw her cigarette down and ground it under her boot. Took an apple out of the sack and stuck out her thumb. C'mon, c'mon.

When she was eleven years old, she had
a dream. She was lying naked and tied
down on the top of a tall stone tower
and a crowd of people were gathered
around the base, staring up at her.
When she awoke, her hand was on her
genitals, the index finger rubbing the
little knob at the apex. She kept on
rubbing and soon felt a very pleasant
spasm, intense and prickly, through
her whole abdomen. Thereafter, she
practised her "trick " several times
a day until her mother came upon her
in the laundry room and her father
whipped his belt across her hands.
She swore violent prayers that she
wouldn't do "it" ever again. Of course,
she did " it " again and again. Sober,
she wondered if she could get cancer
or pregnant. Two seconds after orgasm,
always she was horror-struck.

At two o'clock a '62 Pontiac with a crushed
rear fender screeched to a gravel - spitting stop beside
her and three leering faces and two bottles of beer nodded at her. " Wanna ride? " She waved her arm at them,
meaning " You must be crazy". " Hey! Bitch! " She
stared straight ahead and they drove off, snorting. She
could have a car of her own — who needs this shit? —
if she had a decent job, if she hadn't quit half-way
through second year Arts if she hadn't met James and
that whole crowd. Wow. She could be somewhere
else entirely. Sitting in a library reading books. Getting

a PhD from some grand American university, like Berkeley say. California and the Mendocino Coast or the Big Sur, take your pick. Living alone in a small, Spanish-type cottage on a cliff overlooking the ocean, I dress always in black, I wear my hair long and thick and chunky Aztec jewellery along my arms. About me nothing is known — the local people call me the Queen of Spades — except that every month at full moon I can be seen at the bottom of the cliff, riding my black horse along the shore, my hair and its mane floating in the breeze and the hem of my black cloak dipping in the foam of high tide. And there, a mile away, on the top of the cliff is a man, watching. I know he's there. He's always there. He's black and nameless. I ride on, without desire.

She saw the truck come up the hill, creeping as if in pain, and then heard the air brake as it stopped several yards away from her. She turned around. It didn't move. She picked up the knapsack and trotted over. The guy inside leaned over and pushed open the door on the passenger side. Cross-Cana Freightways, in bright red. Cheerful. She shouted up at him, " How far are you going? " " Brandon." " Terrific. " " So get in. I haven't got all day." She threw her sack and gripping the door frame she hoisted herself way up into the seat and slammed the door, both arms hauling it in. " Thanks." Fifteen gears up again and they were off. Little her on eighteen wheels, half a mile up in the air. She could watch the prairie like a movie in the sideview mirrors.

She learned about the " curse " from a girlfriend whose father worked in a pharmacy. She found the idea nebulously appalling and knew it would never happen to her. When, undressing for bed when she was thirteen, she noticed a dried dark brown stain on the crotch of her panties, she knew, despairingly, disgustedly, the jig was up. She showed the evidence , dangling off her index finger, to her mother who swiftly sequestered her in the bathroom and displayed the equipment that would be part of her undercover life for the next forty years. She sat numbly on the toilet seat while her mother delivered a prepared speech about " from now on ": from now on, during "that time" of the month, she would bathe on her knees, she wouldn't wash her hair, she would sit with her legs shut, she would shave her underarms and legs and would be wise to understand that boys wanted only one thing from her and wiser to withhold it. Her mother walked out and she locked the door after her and howled her chagrin into a towel.

She snuck a look at the driver. About forty, stocky,clean-shaven, blue windbreaker and khaki pants, cowboy boots, a toothpick in his mouth. Hanging off the rear view mirror was a rubber skunk. Cute. Photographs of numerous boys and girls, and a portrait of a middle-aged woman with a deep worry line between her eyebrows, were struck in various slots on the dashboard. Relaxing a little, she leaned back into the corner between the seat and the door and watched the man's big hands move the gearstick like he was playing it. Soon enough she would have to say something but now she simply enjoyed the relief of being in motion again, of getting somewhere beyond the fixed point of the wait on the road. Yeah, this is travelling. Eat up the miles, you big, beautiful rig. Carry me anonymous to somewhere further on. Who will know me there? I can erase all the poses I've struck before. Take a new name. Melissa. Sophie. The Lady Caroline. Sister Johanna of All the Martyrings. In the black wool drapes and white cowl, I walk slipper-footed through Normanesque cloisters, hands folded chastely within the wide sleeves, metal crucifix banging against my bound breasts, a nod to Mother Superior who is spading the ground around the sunflowers in the sororal garden. I enter the room where my visitor waits; I approach the delicate, sculpted wooden screen that separates my territory from his. He is standing with his face pressed against the screen, his hands gripping the bars; I lean against him through the open spaces. Our lips brush each other's face, our fingers coil within the other's hands, I stroke his hair, his hands press against my breasts trying in vain to grip them through the thick cloth, my thigh rubs against the rounded hump of his erection; we are crying. "Johanna, come home!" " I leave you to her." I turn around and walk away, tears streaming down my cheek.

" Is Brandon where you're headed?"

" What?"

" How far are you going? "

" Toronto."

She turned towards him slightly so she could watch him as they talked. He looked straight ahead and glanced into the mirror to watch her eyes whenever he asked a question.

" You got a boyfriend there or something? "

" No."

She avoided his eyes in the mirror.

" Is that your wife? "

" Yeah. She's back in Vancouver."

" Doesn't she get tired of you being on the road all the time? "

" She's used to it. "

" What about your kids? "

" They're growing up."

" Don't you get lonely? "

" I can look after myself. "

They were going up a hill and as he geared down his hand passed over her knee which was propped up near the gearshift. Would she sound churlish to complain? She moved her leg away.

" Relax."

" I am relaxed."

" Don't you ever smile? "

" Only when it's worth it."

" Tough, aren't you? "

He turned his head and grinned at her. It was such an open and boyish grin that she smiled back.

" My oldest is about your age."

" How old do you think I am?"

" Oh, eighteen."

" Wrong."

She laughed, remembering that James had called her " burnt out ".

" Well, you can't be much younger. You're pretty well built."

" What's that got to do with it?"

" Well, you know, you don't expect sixteen year olds to have a chest like that."

He grinned again, glancing sideways at her chest, but she didn't reply. Instinctively she had folded her arms. He lit a cigarette and offered her the pack.

" Help yourself."

" Thanks."

They smoked in silence. She wondered if he was mad at her for not being more fun. She sat up, trying to look sprightly.

" Do you pick up a lot of hitch-hikers? "

" A few. When I'm bored."

" Who's the most interesting one you've picked up? "

He didn't answer right away. Was he even going to bother?

" There was the oldtimer. Said he'd been in the woods for four months."

" Far out."

" Said he just all of a sudden got tired of it, walked to the nearest highway -took him three days- stuck out his thumb. Boy did he stink! "

" How far did you take him? "

" Told him to bugger off at the next filling station."

" Oh."

" Then there was the fifteen year old runaway."

" Where was he going?"

" She. Didn't say."

" Where'd you take her to? "

" She rode with me three days, right to Vancouver. Boy, what a trip that was."

She had no more questions.

" Man oh man, what a trip. You could tell the kid had been around some. Swore like a man and smoked like a chimney and... Said she didn't care where she went, just wanted to hang around with me."

" You could' ve been her father."

He shot a mean look at her.

" So? "

" Forget it. "

" If I hadda been her father, you wouldn't see me let her run around like that, wearing jeans as tight as a snake's skin, language out of a sewer, the morals of a streetwalker."

" Pretty exciting, eh? "

He looked at her puzzled.

" Smart ass."

They pulled off the highway into a service centre. She tried to calculate: was it too late in the day to get another ride, what would she use as an excuse not to rejoin him, was his bark worse than his bite, should she get out while the getting was good, was she being paranoid? In the women's can she flipped a coin. Heads she stayed with him, tails she split.

At seventeen she was going steady and " making love " was contortions in the back seat, wet kisses on her twisted neck and sweating hands plucking ardently at her garters, her waistbands, her hooks and eyes. One night the boy produced a condom from his wallet, tremulously uncoiled it over his penis spread himself over her rigid torso. He ordered her to relax, then to open her legs wider, to follow his rhythm, to open wider for chrissakes. She was conscious of only a lurid shame. When he was still and smiling benignly at her, she said, " You mean that's it? "

It was dusk and they were driving again with styrofoam cups of coffee. He was whistling " Hark the Herald Angels Sing " and she joined in, shyly. He asked her about her home town and told her some stories of getting drunk in the bars there. She told him about quitting school and working as waitress so James could paint. When he turned on the headlights, she talked with more and more detail, drawling out her stories as the space in the cab became cosier. He told her Ukrainian jokes and she laughed. He pulled the truck into a roadside picnic area, turned off the lights and cut off the motor. Her heart sank. He turned to her and put his arm around her shoulders.

" Hey,cut it out."
" Relax."
" I want to keep on going."
" Well I don't. I need a rest."
" That's not what I meant."
" Well, screw what you meant."

She leaned down for her knapsack and put her hand on the door handle. He grabbed her arm and pulled her over to him.

" Not so fast. I thought you liked me."

His free hand was meandering through her hair and down her neck.

" There's a difference between liking —"

His mouth was on hers, a tight-lipped and niggardly kiss. She threw back her head and slammed her hand against his face. He laughed and grabbed at her hair and pulled.

" Okay, okay, you've proved your point. So you're tough. Now how about a little co-operation."

" I'll tell the police."

" Yeah, and I'll tell my mother."

" Let me go! I don't want you! "

Suddenly he released her and, startled, she stared at his crumpled face. She wondered what she had done to him. He gave a deep, piteous sigh and turned to face the steering wheel, his hands in his jacket pockets. She asked him for a cigarette. Gruffly, he told her to help herself. She too sat staring out the front window. She could hear night sounds outside, it was so quiet within the truck. Then, beside her, a rustling and the sound of an undoing zipper. She froze again, alarmed. More rustling and then the soft whacking of a man pulling doggedly at his own penis.

" Lift your t-shirt."

" What?"

" You heard me, bitch. I want to see your tits."

" Leave me out of this."

" You're already in it. I could've raped you, you deserve it, so lift your goddam shirt up! Okay, now turn toward me."

Full of loathing, she stared out the window behind his head, breathing shallowly to keep her breasts still and praying he could make himself come in five seconds flat. Shameless, the sounds he was making, like a barnyard animal, all brainless flesh grunting at a trough. Why me? God in heaven, to be a virgin again, sweetness and innocence, lust deflected by my fragile chastity and the hand that came to appropriate it would curl up in tenderness. Bridal me. Leaning, almost in a swoon, against the bedpost, I watch my groom approach me. I have wrapped myself up in my long, white veil and this he slowly pushes away from me

so that it falls away in a pool at our feet. While his lips
kiss my face, his hands undo the buttons of my dress
and I feel it peel away from my skin like the rind from
an orange. This too lies at our feet, like foam. He is
down on his knees and his mouth travels down my belly
to my thighs. He tells me, an incantation, that I am
lovely, adorable, pure. He presses me down onto the bed
and slides one stocking and then the other off my legs.
His hands are inside my panties, the fingernails digging
into my buttocks. I am trembling, I am fainting.

" Now get out."

He was wiping his hand on a handkerchief and
stuffing himself back inside his pants.

" You said you'd take me to Brandon."

" I said I was going to Brandon. I never said
I'd take you there. Now get your ass outta here. "

" Aw, c'mon. It's nighttime. It's cold out there."

"Scram."

" Pig."

She opened the door and hauled the knapsack
out with her as she jumped to the ground. He pulled it
shut behind her and took off. She stood screaming at
the sky. " You bastard! You disgusting animal!
Fascist!" And went to lie down under a picnic table
and fall asleep, murder in her heart.

She settled down by setting up house
with an artist, happy to withdraw from
the sexual bazaar she had been trading
in. Exhausted by fly-by-night affairs
and her merchant's need to guarantee
satisfaction to even the most spurious
customer, she accepted James and do-

mestic ordinariness. But the rules of
commerce bound her still. She and
James would to to bed and they would
make love and every time, unfailingly,
he would ask, " Did you come?" with a
puppy's eagerness so that every time
she would answer, " yes ". It kept the
peace.

I am walking into a big room, a salon in the
eighteenth -century European style and the doors shut
silently behind me. I pause. I am a presence. Slowly
everyone in the room turns to watch me as I begin to
walk down the passage; their bodies open for me. My
golden hair is piled in thick waves around my head,
my skin is luminous, the silk stockings around my
thighs swish against each other and I dangle a rose
from my hand. I am looking straight ahead, although
all eyes are upon me, and I can feel the rising desire
in all the men around me like steam from a bath. I
am unmoved. Their most poetic fantasies cannot chase
the chill from my heart. I walk out of the room alone
and unpossessed. Well, will you look at her. Strutting
down the highway with her thumb stuck out, lonesome
on the open road.

COLUMBUS HITS THE SHORELINE RAG

Candas Jane Dorsey

"... and the fiddler played a tune
at a quarter past noon
called ' Columbus Hits the Shoreline Rag'..."

A. Fraser

WHAT DO YOU SEE WHEN YOU TURN OUT THE LIGHT? (a bay in the New World)
I was down below the edge of the world and looking for a way back up when Isabella called me, she said

alright, let's get some action here
what's bugging you, baby?
About time we cleared up this flat earth crap
so she put me on a ship and tripped me off to foreign climes and that's how I got where I am today.
Isabella thinks I found it on purpose, of course.

She doesn't know how much time I was spending in the after stores consoling myself with the storeskeeper, a tubercular young man who fortuitously looked a great deal like the girl I had been forced to leave behind me—well, you know, it's the same old sad story, and that's where I was when the cry went up and the crash came.

I emerged on deck quite *deshabillé* to realize that the ship was no longer moving, that tedious cresting and troughing, in point of fact we had run aground, and all sorts of quite bizarre really and rather naked personnages were clustered around the bow making savage-sounding chitchat which I was totally unable to decipher. I sent the cabin boy (he'd do anything for me) down to my quarters for the universal translator and gradually it all came clear to me—

    wow

    far out

    What IS that?

    must be a UFO

    never saw an unidentified floating object quite that big

    Suppose those are real people?

    nah, it's all done with holographs

    yeah, when I was up in Disney World last winter, you know the stuff up there you just wouldn't

    Hey, that one's saying something

    far out, they talk too! And the lips are in synch

    Don't be stupid, it must be real. Have you ever seen an illusion with its fly undone

    —so I pulled myself together and made some speech or other and then I saw this quite luscious young thing on the edge of the crowd dressed in really a rather informal way and of course the crew was restless after all that time on the roving main so to speak so I de-

clared shore leave for the whole fleet (the other ships
by this time having anchored in the bay).

Well. You can't imagine the way the men
cheered, and the natives, after a moment

(well, I never, just like that, without a by-your-
leave

I bet they don't even ask before they raid the
fridge either)

were quite complimentary—

Suppose we should Make Welcome

guess so

Chief?

after you my dear councillor

why not have some young person give an appropriate

of course my lovely daughter would be more
than happy to

oh mother!

do what I tell you, girl

(oh all right) O wayfarers from the lands far
away across the sea we the people of these united is-
lands welcome you in the name of etcetera etcetera and
invite you to share with us the fruits of our land

(at this the storeskeeper looked interested)

the game on our table

(what game? said the second mate

blackjack of course, only game in town, re-
plied a councillor, *sotto voce* as we say at home)

the hospitality of our yurts and so forth. Do
please disembark from yon bark

(of course all the men by this time had leaped
overboard onto the sand)

and have ye a great old time, taking proper pre-
cautions while doing thereso as we have stabilized the

birthrate and are trying very hard to maintain a balanced post-transitional ecology.

—and who could refuse an offer like that?
         It was while they were putting together the bacon sandwiches and we were passing out the carbonated drinks that the mate, a chummy sort of fellow really, went to the chief and asked her for her daughter's hand in marriage, the chief by this time quite soused on palm wine—

         of course of course take all of her why don't you !

         stupid foreigners
         -- and as Captain of course I was approached to make with the dearly beloved we are gathered in order that they might then go off and consummate their union (I having during this time absorbed in the exploration of new territory in the shape of the lovely morsel I'd seen in the welcoming crowd)
         however
         I recognized in the chief's daughter a certain resemblance to a girl I'd left pining in Barcelona and finding a spirit of co-operation lacking in the young thing I'd first found
         (get your paws off me you old fleabag)
         I sent it packing and ordered the mate back to the ship to stand watch
         but Cap, he said
         no buts I said accurate as usual as Sir Walter hadn't been invented yet
         No no a thousand times she cried
         but I was developing an acute case of *droit de seigneur* and in the end

TOUGH TITTY SAID THE KITTY BUT THE MILK'S
ALRIGHT (an island, ibid)

It was not long afterward that I was approached
in my palm frond hut by the head of the Social Anthro-
pology team, to discuss a matter of cultural import.

Seems our closely (but apparently insufficient-
ly) monitored shore leave was tending to disrupt the
natural tribal patterns of the natives to such an extent
that they were finding serious strictures beginning to
affect the ordering of their reality such that the estab-
lished ethical constructs which had sustained their cul-
ture through the demographic transition and centuries
of other difficulties were degenerating into an unpre-
cedented shock reaction which if left to continue would
tend to halt their hitherto unchecked forward evolution
and place their society among the ranks of endangered
social systems within a short period of time.

moreover the chief herself appeared to make a
statement about the prevailing social climate

you have to get your disreputable crew out of
here! And quit handling my daughter! Haven't you got
any respect for our taboos? None of you gives a fig
about

I really couldn't see what they all expected me
to do about it considering that the seed had already
been planted in more ways than one, and I myself in
any case have always been in favour of the melting pot
of society concept over the idea of maintaining cultural
integrity, so with my free hand I waved them away

but, said the chief still lingering in the doorway,
we've never done things this way

Tough titty, I said, continuing to caress her
daughter lewdly, and motioning for the security team.
Shove off.

And eventually we did.

WHAT DID YOU BRING ME FROM AMERICA DADDY? (Spain, some time later)
>Chris, how lovely
>isn't she
>I mean, to see you. Who is she?
>The lawful wedded widow of my first mate. I've been showing her around Barcelona
>she must be bringing in the ducats
>oh, she does. Would you like her, Izzy?
>Thank you so much! Where did you get her ? America
>so you cleared up this nonsense about the edge of the edge of the world being just over the continental shelf
>sure did. You proud of me?
>oh, Chris, you know I am. What else did you find there?
>Well. The natives have some simply charming customs, let me show you
>splendid! and when we get up we can hurry and discover tobacco and claim new lands and so forth
>but in the meantime
>(MUSIC. VIOLINS)

LIFE IS MUCH MORE FUN WHEN YOU'RE REFRESHED (San Salvador)
>You're WHAT?
>By who?
>Those whiteskinned barbarians?
>don't give me that

well at least your sister didn't
What's that you're mixing with your palm wine?
Coca what Company?
    (Dear Sirs. Please be advised that in accordance
with accepted Foreign Policy and based on Information
rec'd from various Explorers in the Region,
    (I have hereby claimed these Islands, heretofore
to be known as San Salvador, and all those lands which
Lie beyond, in the name of the King and Queen and the
Sovereign Nation and So On, and do hereby establish
thereon this Colony,
    (hoping you will see fit to send sundry Troops
to hold the Settlement and for the Protection of the
Natives

I REMEMBER THE WINTER OF '92 (woodlands of
— later — Alberta)
    I was down below the edge of the world when
the news came, I was lying under birch trees, let me tell
you about the world
    was sunshine and high summer
    many fish in streams
    my mother soaking bark in the sunwarmed
water curving it into baskets
    my father and father's brother gone to the
prairie after buffalo
    o yes it was one idyllic scene, all right. Those
days will never come again, little one
    I was looking thru leaves at the sky and a hawk
was circling, was thinking O what a beautiful morning
o what a beautiful day! He was wearing next to nothing
(our habit in those days) running down the path

breathless
he said Hey!

whaa?

Hey, he said, hey! and I realized he was gasping
and gave him some water and a neckrub and presently
he said

america has been discovered
oh, I said, where?
Here, he said

who done it? (my phrasing was classical)

hell, they say some Vikings popped in genera-
tions ago, but it's a bunch of Spaniards making the news
now. I understand they're making a big fuss about the
whole thing, and they're a real bunch of degenerates
too, I'm told

He took off his loincloth to mop his sweaty
brow and I said

well, that's it, then
I'm afraid so
how long have we got?

they won't get here in our lifetime, but we'd
better teach the kids a thing or two. Mind you, there
may be compensations. Already they've introduced
some stange new customs into the civilized world,
shall I show you?

I hardly know you
I'm your uncle's brother-in-law's cousin's son

from the sociologically differentiated tribe
down the valley?

indeed
and these customs?
very interesting I think

So I turned off the universal translator and we
communicated more subtly after that.

MY NAME IS OZYMANDIAS, KING OF KINGS
(Batoche, centuries later)

    ouch

    dammit, what now

    I stubbed my toe, Daddy. On that nasty rock

    That's not a rock, dear, it's an artifact

    An artifact? You stubbed your toe on a goddamn artifact? An how much is that going to cost me ?

    oh, hush, Ed, it's not broken

    well, just pick up your feet

    how come we're stopping here anyhow, Daddy?

    There was some big Indian battle or something here.

    Red Indians, Daddy?

    don't bother your daddy now, dear. The bus ride made him feel sick

    mommy, I have to go to the bathroom

    you'll have to wait for the bus to come back

    but mommy, why?

    there are no bathrooms here, this is a historic site

    think we can see it all in twenty minutes, sylvia?

    it'll have to be a quickie

    I hate these package tours

SET THE CONTROLS FOR THE HEART OF THE SUN (the end)

    I was down below the edge of the world when the call came, looking at the way back, I flipped the switch and the voice said

    request permission to come

granted

aboard

sure (you see, I'd been having these dreams—)

and in they came, sifting thru the computer
banks looking none the worse for wear right from that
first sad darkskinned beauty down to the intense
Canadian kid with the big voice and I said hi welcome
siddown as they kept coming, figuring it was near the
end of the flight and when I was sick of the illusion
they'd all go away, maybe be replaced by some of the
tanned lovelies I saw in Florida when I was training,
o the nights at the Copacabana Motel, but no, an orbit
and a half later they were all still there, so crowded
I was starting to worry about the oxygen, and not as
transparent as they'd been at first, for of course by
then they'd gone thru a good deal of past history, mur-
muring between themselves, and a good deal of my
dehydrated food—

tastes like pemmican, said AV

been a long time, eh? said a woman

—and all the time looking at me just a little
bit oddly—

I think we took them too seriously

you're not one to talk, Long Lance

well, you let them put you through school, so

It's all a matter of whose reality triumphs (that
was the old man in the white shirt and pants)

but he looks so real (the first woman)

of course I am, it's you people who are the big
dream. Why don't you buzz off, anyhow? It's almost
time for me to start re-entry

—looking at me oddly, and then they started
playing with the switches, not fading away at all, and
finally Mission Control called up (I always like that

phrase) called up (everything is relative anyhow)
called up and said what the hell are you doing up there
playing button button? your brain wave monitors have
gone crazy, your payload has increased, however the
hell you managed that, you've just left orbit, and you've
hit the manual override, so we can't take over from you.
Have you finally gone bonkers? Pull yourself together!
and one of them grabs the mike and it's—

Ermineskin here, friend. Just call me chief
—what?—
A few of us decided to come on up here and get
into the action
right on
shhh
and we're wondering what there is to discover
up here
—whaa?—
After all, you discovered us, now it's our turn
Right!
shhh
— come off it, how are you doing all those different voices?—
We are (he continued, reading from a hide
handed to him — thanks, Long Lance) we are the vic-
tims of overwhelming cultural genocide and we have
at the last possible moment rallied and have decided to
make the biggest gesture of our collective career and this
particular cooperative international endeavour is just the
right vehicle. So if you'd kindly lay on the media
coverage we can get on with it.
—That's all very well said Mission Control but
at the moment your fancy fingerwork has screwed up
the course so much that if you don't get that astronaut
back in control the whole damn thing's gonna burn right

up and then where will you be o noble savage and all
that? Not to speak of hijacking and kidnapping and how
the hell you got up there in the first place—

that was uncalled for said AV and cut the com-
munications off, then thought better of it and grabbed
the headset, turned on the switch and began crooning
wordlessly into the mike

hey, what are you, I said, and he looked at me
oddly. Again.

Wadddya think, pasteface, I'm chanting. Tra-
dition has it that

They're just a big delusion! Just ignore them,
Mission Control, come in Mission Control, they'll go
away eventually, you know these dreams I've been
having, it's all just a

Shut up, man, you're screwing up my song
dream, there aren't any Indians up here, none at
could somebody get this nuisance out of here?
(one with an American accent)

The way to deal with us is not by ignoring us
(this was the one in the rusty black suit, Ermineskin had
called him Long Lance). That just exacerbates the prob-
lem. I'm preparing a long statement for the wire
services. You may be interested in the analysis I make of
the cultural precedents for, and factors leading up to,
our present actions. You know, there was a time when I
really thought we could work with you people, but now
I

c'mon, man, cool it

look, Voice, this celebration song business can
go too far. We haven't even gotten started. Besides, I
need the mike to read my press release.

shit, man, I was just getting into it! What kind of
an Indian are you anyways?

I'm with you all the way, you know that, we dis-
cussed all this

Haven't you all received enough recognition in
the last few years to make up for it? I said trying to grab
AV's arm my hands sliding thru like wind

besides, you may find us as capable of ignoring
you, and you will become the history which never happened (the one with the Spanish accent)

—Mission Control calling, Mission Control
calling, acknowledge, acknowledge—

can't you hear that?

man, I can only hear Cree

—acknowledge, important course correction in
three minutes, three minutes, C minus three minutes and
counting, mark, are you there, acknowledge—

that so? I'm a Yaqui, myself

Iroquois

can't you hear (I feel myself getting hysterical)
listen, if you don't let me make that correction we'll

don't sweat it, man, relax. You're coming apart
anyhow. Gitchie Manitou'll take care of it

burn up, listen to me, what is it you people want
anyhow? Can't you

AV, I think you've got a great idea, let's all sing
a bit of a

listen to me! Don't you know we're not the same
ones? You can't blame us for what some sixteenth cen-
tury barbarians did! We can't be responsible for the mistakes of our forefathers

don't forget foremothers, there

aaaaaaaaahhhhhhhhh, ahhahhohhhooohhh

don't you know that all the astronauts in the Canadian space program except me are Caughnawaga Mohawks,

nobody else can stand the heights, what more do you

oh, shut up, man, we've had it with your buzzing

you're all going to die, what kind of a dumb gesture is that, why don't you just hit that remote switch there, see, I'll let you do it all by yourselves, no interference from a white person, then you'll get all the credit, isn't that enough of a

what's that funny humming noise, man?

oh, nothing, Voice, just ignore it and it'll go away

Long Lance, you said you could work with us

(Not now, sorry, I've chosen the Indian way. I've gone too far now. Happy trails) What's that tune, Geronimo? Cochise? Ermine?

—Mission Control calling! Course correction minus ten seconds and counting, nine,eight—

What's that red light, Juan?

that's not important. Keep singing

hey, what's happening to me, what's

—five, four, three—

Say, this is far out, eh, Long Lance? Look at that view

It certainly is a giant step for the Indian Confederacy. Capital idea of yours, Voice

Thanks, man. Hey, look at that

—Mission Control calling, please acknowledge, you have missed course correction, please jettison pod, jettison immediately, rescue mission is ready for launch, jettison immediately, you are in dangerous proximity to the sun's gravitational field, you are in dangerous—

hey,man, look how close we are!

wow

Far out!

Let's get that counterpoint going again, people, c'mon

ahhhaayyahhaayyy

—proximity to the sun—

It seems to be warming up some, Spotted Calf

Sure is, Big Bear. Just breathe deep and keep chanting

I hereby claim this Fiery Ball in the name of the Indian Sovereign Nations and do give it the Name of Sun, Life-Giver, and do here establish the first Colony in the name of all Brothers and Sisters of our Nations and of the Gitchie Manitou, by whatever name each calls the Spirit

Hey, Ermie, it's getting hot in here, man, isn't there any more water?

Just relax, Voice, keep chanting, it'll be alright soon, everything'll be okay as soon as we

PRINCESS

Terese Brasen

Mother kneaded the bread dough, pounding it with her wrists, turning it over and over with a slow, solemn rhythm that reminded Maria of prayer.

" Remember the garden? " she said, pausing to stare out the window. Memory washed over her like happiness. She seemed oblivious to the cement patios and the parking lot, to the grey, stucco, row houses that her window faced; as though her window opened onto an imaginary past.

" How I miss the garden," she said. " The lilacs. The raspberries. Do you remember the garden Maria?"

Maria stood by the kitchen sink with her back at right angles to Mother. She poured boiling water into a glass bowl over a package of red, raspberry jell-o. The powder dissolved into color. The smell burnt her nostrils like bleach fumes. Maria remembered the garden. Early in the morning she would weave her way

through the thorny raspberry hedge, filling the red bowl
with berries for breakfast. Maria didn't always know
that she was remembering the garden; but that feeling
of wanting to be somewhere else was always there, inside her, like a distraction.

"But it's a good thing," Mother said finally
with downcast eyes. "It's a good thing that we live
here. I have enough work to overcome without a garden."

Maria lived on the outskirts of the city. The
row houses were fenced in by a tall, wooden struc-
ture with only one exit that seemed way too far away.
Maria and Sharon, both acrobats, climbed the fence
daily and walked along it. They balanced the tenuous
height even when the laughing wind tested them,
swaying the fence from side to side.

From the fence they saw both sides. On the
city side the row houses regulated the landscape like a
mathematical equation. The row houses consisted of
eight rectangles, arranged on a rectangular grid, and margined on all four sides by a paved road. The rectangles,
separated by grass areas and by parking lots, were di-
vided into squares. Each square belonged to one family.
To the front, facing the grass area, each square had one
brown picture window on ground level, and two smaller
night-time windows on the upper level.

Maria's square faced Sharon's. Their night-time
windows faced each other. If Maria turned off her bedroom light, she could see across into Sharon's room. She
could see Sharon: a silhouette behind an uncurtained
window.

On the other side of the fence—fields of crab
grass, thigh-high dandelions, wild oats looking like

corn in the sun, wild strawberries, bushes trying to be
trees, forever and ever... The wilderness seemed to continue even past the edge where the field and sky folded
to touch each other.

" I don't want you going out there," Maria's
Mother warned. " That's where bad girls go. And think
what would happen if you fell climbing that fence."
Maria did think about falling, falling hard against the
cement sidewalk or falling into a field of sun-yellow
dandelions. Maria had a sense of her preference, but
only a sense. Mother had a thing about dandelions.

" Dandelions are weeds," she would say. " Flowers grow in flower beds. That's why we like them.
Dandelions grow everywhere. If we're not careful, the
whole world will be dandelions."

2

Mother wasn't feeling well. She was upstairs
in her room convalescing over *The Lives of the Saints*.
Marc too was upstairs in his room, his headquarters,
brooding over *Mein Kampf*. Maria wound up the vacuum cleaner cord. She had wiped the dust off the
television, off the piano, off the bookshelves until the
air was so thick with dust that the windows had to be
opened. The supernatural dust, the boredom, that clung
eternally to the clock and the carpet and the corners of
the house was impossible, it seemed, to vacuum or wipe
away.

It was still early. The Saturday comics wouldn't
arrive until four in the afternoon. Maria was making
a path towards the refrigerator thinking about radishes
and green onions when the door bell rang. Through the

screen mesh of the door, Maria distinguished Sharon's
face: a pair of brown eyes peering out frantically from
behind a curtain of bangs. Dean, the youngest of her
brothers, mud-faced and dirty-diapered, clung to
Sharon's leg.

" She's got Dean's shoes," Sharon spit out.
" The witch's got Dean's shoes. He went down there
and she come chasing him with her cane. 'Get out of
here you brat!' she was screaming at him, and he lost
his shoes. His shoes fell off and they're still out there."
Sharon spewed out the words so fast she was short of
breath. " He hasn't got any other shoes. Mom'll kill
him if she finds out. We've got to get them back before
she gets back."

The rectangular shadows of the row houses
etched the sidewalk and the grass area. When they
passed through the exit, the world opened, revealing
an expnase of blue sky and an array of golden grasses,
mainly dandelions, that rose to meet the sky. In the
centre of the field where the earth stooped to the
lowest, and where the dandelions grew the highest, in
a grey house misshapen by time, lived an old stoop-
backed woman who hid all but her face under a black
shawl. When she came into the city, rowing herself
along the sidewalk with her gnarled cane, the children
ran, ran without looking back until they were out of her
sight. The old woman had lived in the wild country long
before fences, and long before the earth had been regulated by houses and margined by streets.

As they walked, the wild oats **parted**, swinging
back, tickling their bare knees and thighs.

" She's not a witch," Maria said. Her voice was
as sudden an interruption as the butterfly that flounced

by. The butterfly had red stripes on its wings. " She's only a stupid, old lady, probably more scared of us than we of her." Then the grey boards began, leading down to the witch's house.

Maria wanted to turn back.

" Let's go, " Sharon said.

" No," Maria said.

" Come on, " Sharon said, pulling Maria's arm. arm.

Maria said three Hail Marys and knocked on the witch's door. She knocked again. Still there was no answer. Then the door creaked open. There the woman stood: her shrivelled face, her eyes grey with age, her figure planted like resistance in the doorway.

" Ah...we lost a pair of shoes this morning," Maria said. " It was an accident. We didn't mean to be trespassing but Dean, Sharon's brother, lost his shoes." The woman's face showed no understanding. " We lost some shoes," Maria repeated.

" No shoes." The woman shook her head. " No shoes." Her words fell like stones from her mouth, fell down her rounded body, and rolled down the porch at Maria and Sharon. Maria and Sharon tried to ma- nouevre glances past the woman into the house. Per- haps she was hiding Dean's shoes. A bag of potatoes leaned against the leg of a makeshift, wooden table. Chairs balanced on the uneven floors. The door shut in their faces.

Maria and Sharon followed the grey boards away from the house, until the oats and the dandelions met them like a sea of weeds.

" I don't want you going out there," Maria's Mother had warned, turning a knife around a potato with her determined hands. " That's where bad men go. And think what could happen to two girls all alone out there."

Maria didn't care about Dean's shoes. She only wanted an excuse to go out *there*. She couldn't remember seeing Dean with shoes on. All day long he sat digging up the grass area outside Sharon's picture window, smearing the dirt all over himself, eating the dirt.

" Dirt's good for him, " Sharon explained to Maria. " It's got minerals."

The brown fence swayed back and forth drawing a curved line against the sky, hiding the row houses, the patios and the parking lots so cleverly that Maria and Sharon dusted away any lingering thoughts about mothers and brothers and witches and shoes. They walked in a trance. The yellow sun melted over them. A breeze combed the weeds. A butterfly flounced by. Then it re-appeared. They caught a glimpse of it through the poplar trees. They walked towards it. Silver-blue, it mirrored the empty sky. They stood at the shore of the muddy slough. They hung their heads over trying to see the bottom, but water gave only changing, distorted reflections.

3

One upon a time Maria lived in a happy house with a large garden. In the summer the smells were as clear as voices. Daytime was all about eating: eating peas and rhubarb and raspberries.

This was the garden that Mother remembered. This was the garden that Mother found too much work, especially with on one to help with the potatoes and dandelions. Mother grew more and more afraid that the garden would go to seed, and grow wild with dandelions. Mother cried. Father phoned the moving van. Maria packed her dolls. Marc packed his model airplanes. Mother phoned the Salvation Army. Maria and Marc would tell by the determination in Mother's fingers as she tied the string around the boxes, that they would never come back to the garden. When Maria closed her eyes, she could feel as though she was there again in that house, looking out her window at the garden.

From her bedroom window Maria watches the sunrise. Way far away, way past all the houses and the grocery stores, Maria sees a line of fir trees silhouetted against a wash of Easter egg purple. The trees outside her window make a small wind. The garden vegetables shake their heads, stretch and yawn as they see morning coloring the sky. Morning is a secret time. Birds sing. People snore. Mr. White takes his Labrador for a walk.

The hardwood stretches under Maria's feet. The door yawns open. The tap screams morning. Maria takes the big red bowl outside. Crossing the dewy grass, she finds herself again at the raspberry hedge. She holds her hand under a raspberry leaf, letting an over-ripe berry fall into her warm palm. She tries to hold it without squishing it, but it is no use. The raspberry juice colors her palm. Standing carefully with bare legs in thorny bushes, Maria tilts back her head, closes her eyes and lets the raspberry, tasting life forever, fall into her. The taste soaks into her like a stain. She is careful not to disturb the humming birds and the butterfly with tiger-striped wings. She wants to stand in the raspberry hedge forever, but her body is an intruder. Her body is like

time moving into forever. Morning becomes daytime.
Maria's bowl becomes full. Traffic, like conversation, in-
terrupts the silence of the streets. The flowers along the
house open their buds and smile at Maria. The screen
door shuts behind her.

Maria listens for the sound of silver on china,
for the sound of a cup meeting a saucer. She waits for
the smell of coffee. She thinks about telling Mother and
Father about the butterfly with its tiger-striped wings.
She can feel her voice becoming excited. She sets the
red bowl on the counter. Mother is not there making
coffee. There are no cups and saucers on the table.
The house feels unhappy like those mornings when
Father takes his brown suitcase and goes to Saskatchewan on business, and Mother cries because fourteen
days seem like forever. The house feels grey and empty.

"Maria," Father says. His voice is low and holy
like Father Sullivan's when Father Sullivan recites the
Hail Marys at Benediction. Father is in the living room,
sitting on the sofa. He is dressed for work, but his shirt
collar is unbuttoned and his tie is loose. Maria has never
felt this tall, standing in the entrance way, before.

" Come here," Father says.

" Where's Mom?" Maria says.

" Come here and sit on my lap."

" Where's Mom?"

" I drove her to the hospital."

" You're lying," Maria says, angrily.

" Last night."

" What? "

" I drove her to the hospital last night."

" You're lying," Maria says. She runs into
Mother's bedroom. She searches the closets. She runs
down to the laundry room, runs outside, hoping to find

Mother at the lilac hedge gathering flowers.

Father isn't lying. Mother is in the hospital. She may stay there forever. When Father leaves for work, Maria takes out Mother's vacuum cleaner. She feels so much older. She thinks about cooking supper. She thinks about Mother. Mother doesn't have time to be anywhere forever.

At early morning Masses Father, Marc and Maria prayed for Mother. Maria thought that Mother would die. Maria asked the Holy Virgin to make Maria strong enough to be the new mother.

Every morning Maria watched the sunrise, later with each day, until the lilac bushes lost their flowers and turned rust-brown; until all the vegetables were dug up, and the garden was left black and empty; until the trees were scraggly branches outside her window. Then the snow came streaking her window. Then the snow blanketed the garden. Maria pressed her face against the glass and thought about the butterflies and humming birds frozen into forever.

When Mother came home Maria thought Mother was dead. Her virgin-blue eyes bulged from her head. Her hair was thin and fly away, and reminded Maria of a halo. She was too fat for her old clothes. She only wore her blue dress, the one that reminded Maria of nighttime.

Mother kept her pills in an egg cup on the window sill.

" If I don't take my pills I will die," Mother told Maria.

" If you take them will you get better?" Maria asked.

" I hope so," Mother said.

" I hope so too, " Maria said.

Maria was already tired of being Mother, tired of vacuuming and dusting and cooking.

4

" Will Maria always be my little princess?" Father would say holding Maria on his lap.

" I'll always, always be your princess," Maria would say, hugging Father as though he was silly to ask such questions.

In the mornings, Maria would kneel beside Mother who sat in the red, sofa chair, twisting Maria's hair into long braids, pulling the tiny hairs at the back of Maria's neck so tight Maria wanted to scream. Maria wanted to let her yellow-white hair hang down over her shoulders, but Mother said it would always be falling in Maria's face and that school was not the place to be thinking about hair. Even then, Maria thought that Mother wanted to make her ugly.

The green canvas blinds are pulled halfway down African violets and coleus line the shelf below the window. Outside, the play area is a blanket of snow. Hoarfrosted trees reach for the empty sky. Maria is studying feet. Seven people are wearing running shoes. Most people are pigeon-toed.

Mrs. Macintyre announces the Christmas play. The play is to be about a king who meets a princess and takes her for a wife. Mrs. Macintyre admits that the play doesn't have anything to do with Christmas, but when she was a girl her school performed the play, and she played the part of the princess.

Mrs. Macintyre stands in front of the classroom

in the shadow of a canvas blind. Arms akimbo she shifts weight from side to side. Her legs are like matchsticks. Her hair is like a crown, curled up high with two symmetrical kiss curls on either side of her forehead. In the mornings the curls are stiff with hair spray; but by afternoon, she has said, " I'm sick, sore and tired," so many times her curls droop down her forehead.

" Who will volunteer to be the king?" she asks playing with her loose, accordian neck.

" Pasquali," everyone, except Pasquali, yells. Pasquali is fat. No one else would do such a sissy thing.

When Mrs. Macintyre asks for volunteers for the princess, Maria looks down at her desk. It is better to be picked. Who else could Mrs. Macintyre pick? There is Wendy who wears glasses scotch taped at the sides and pees her pants. There is Theresa who is taller than any of the boys, especially Pasquali.

No one volunteers.

" Volunteer," Tim whispers. Tim sits in front of Maria. His hair is shaved in a brush cut and the back of his head is as flat as a board. Mother explained to Maria, when she asked, that Tim's mother laid him on his back when he was a baby. Maria is proud of her egg-shaped head.

" Me?" Maria says pretending surprises. " You'd have to memorize so many line."

" So you might get to kiss Pasquali," Tim says poking her with his pencil. Maria blushes plum-red.

" Well," Mrs. Macintyre says, playing with her red button earring and smacking her red lips together. " If no one wants to volunteer, I'll have to pick someone." Her eyes scan the rows of desks as though trying to find a number in the telephone book. " It will have to be someone who can memorize."

Maria is the best in the class at memorizing. She can spit out the answers to the catechism questions faster than anyone else can read them. In the evenings, Maria sits beside Father in the double bed. Their backs propped up with pillows, they practise spelling and catechism until Maria feels very smart and very special. Sometimes, when they finish early, they lie beside each other, rubbing noses, the way the Eskimos do.

" But it will have to be someone deserving," Mrs. Macintyre continues. " Someone with good grades and few absentees. Catherine, how would you like to be the princess? "

CATHERINE HOW WOULD YOU LIKE TO BE THE PRINCESS?

The words explode inside Maria. Catherine who can't read in front of the class without crying. Catherine without any lips. Without any voice. Without any hair.

Even then, Maria knew it was Mother's fault. It was Mother who braided Maria's hair, who made her wear darned tights and shoes with laces. Mother wanted Maria to be just as ugly as Mother.

5

When Maria lived in the house with the garden, she had a friend named Diane. Diane was a lot like Sharon, except Diane had nice clothes and always knew her spelling.

Maria was in grade four when she decided to become a nun. Mrs. Macintyre thought it was a good idea. So did

Mother. Mother had always hoped that Maria would
find such a vocation. On Halloween she dressed Maria
up as The Virgin. When Maria reached across the table,
Mother would say, " The Holy Virgin would never reach
across the table." When Maria yelled, " Shut up!" at
Marc, Mother would say, " The Holy Virgin would never
yell 'shut up!' "

Father thought Maria's decision was a shame.
Wouldn't Maria have to cut off all her beautiful, yellow
hair?

Maria practised. At supper she ate only half as
much. She never ate cake. She slept without her pillow.
But Maria was always falling into temptation. She was
always yelling, " Shut up!" at Marc.

" The Holy Virgin was born without original
sin. She never once told a lie," Mother explained. " She
never once wanted to sin." Maria knew she had original
sin. She had evidence. But she felt she could overcome
it. She overcame all those other obstacles that gave
people problems. Like waking up in the morning. Like
arithmetic. Like catechism questions. Like double-dutch
skipping.

It was one Thursday late in May that Maria first
decided, definitely, no turning back, to give her whole
life to God. On her eighteenth birthday she would shave
off all her yellow hair, and never wear a red dress or red
shoes again until she got to heaven.

One old man who wears a straw hat is always
trimming his hedge when they walk by in late afternoon.

" Hi boys. What did you learn in school today?"
he always says. Maria never answers. Mother has taught
her not to talk to strange men. " They offer little girls
ice cream cones, then drive them out to the country,

and do bad things to them."

Maria and Diane break caragana blossoms off the hedges as they walk   along. They jump hopscotches. From the moon to mars on one leg without stepping on any lines. Diane sings skipping songs as she twirls the wound up skipping rope in her hand.

"Grapes on the vine ready to be picked. One fell down, and the other did the splits."

"Should we do it today?" Diane asks.

"Do you want to?" Maria asks.

"If you do," Diane says.

"I will if you will," Maria says.

"O.K." Diane says.

"What if somebody sees us?" Maria asks.

"No one will," Diane says.

"But what if?" Maria asks.

"God sees us," Diane says thoughtfully.

"Think so?" Maria asks thoughtfully.

"He sees everything," Diane says. "We could go to hell."

"Only if it's a mortal sin," Maria says.

"I think it's venial," Diane says.

"So do I," Maria says.

"But it could be mortal," Diane says.

"My mother would think it's mortal," Maria decides.

"So would mine and Mrs. Macintyre," Diane agrees.

"But grown-ups," Maria says.

"Not my mother," Diane says.

"Or mine," Maria says.

"I'll do it when I grow up," Diane says.

"So will I," Maria says. "Unless I become a

nun."

"Me too," Diane agrees.

They turn into the alley. Each yard is fenced by trees. They stop by a garbage can. They look down the valley. No one is coming. Maria slides down her panties and bends over, lifting her dress. Diane kisses Maria three times on her bum. Then it is Maria's turn. She gives Diane three quick kisses. Diane pulls up her panties and runs. Maria runs down the alley towards home, blushing all the way. What if anyone found out? What if Diane told her mother? What if they got pregnant?

Maria decided never to do it again. She didn't want to dirty her soul. She decided to tell Diane that she didn't want to get pregnant, and that she wanted to be a nun. All night she prayed, asking God to help her with her decision. "Oh my God I am heartily sorry for having offended thee..." she prayed over and over until she felt that her soul was clean.

From her bedroom window Maria watches the sunrise. She can see the edge of the world, way past all the houses and grocery stores, where the sky meets the earth. Maria does not go out into the garden. She kneels by her bed. She prays three Hail Marys. She dresses in her yellow princess dress and her wide brimmed Sunday hat with the cloth flowers and wide yellow ribbon.

Down the quiet streets in the lemon sunlight. The sound of her footsteps on the sidewalk. Choirs of birds in the trees. The hum of distant traffic. The sky looking like forever.

Inside, clean sunlight eases through the stained glass windows. The church is almost empty. There are only older people kneeling in the occasional pew, saying their private prayers. Maria kneels close to the altar across from Mrs. Dominiki. Mrs. Dominiki kneels through out the Mass. Her eyes burn like the saints' in the holy pictures. She has visions. She has not even lost her faith since her husband died suddenly of arteriosclerosis. Maria envies Mrs. Dominiki for being so close to the glorious whiteness that comes after death.

Maria asks God to make her a saint. She says special prayers to the Virgin. She concentrates on the host as the priest holds it high. At communion she bows her head and prays fervently. Coming back from communion, walking with slow steps, head bowed, hands folded, she feels it. A sharp burning pain in her heart. Like God's holy arrow. She knows. God has chosen her.

After the Mass on the front steps of the church, Maria stands considering the long day ahead of her. A shaking hand touches hers. From under a black shawl Mrs. Dominiki's face peers. Her skin is pulled over sharp bones. Her holy eyes burn. Her lips crinkle into a smile. " My child you make God happy," Mrs. Dominiki says. " You are his little one."

Down the stairs. Down the sidewalk. Waving her arms. Stopping for a moment to pull up her knee socks and fix her Sunday hat. Maria thanks God. " Always, always will I be yours," she whispers.

Maria kneels inside the confessional.

" Bless me Father for I have sinned. It has been one week since my last confession. Since then I have yelled at my brother seven times, stolen money from my mother's purse and told two lies."

" Say three Hail Marys and one Our Father."

The screen divider slides shut. Maria's turn is over.

Marc paints mustaches on Maria's dolls. " You stupid girl," he says all the time. " Shut up!" Maria yells back all the time. Marc tempts Maria, making her sin. Marc is the devil.

Father is in Saskatchewan on a business trip. Mother and Marc and Maria are having supper. Stew from a can. Mother dishes some onto Maria's plate. Grey-brown lumps of meat and carrots.

" I'm not eating cowboy food," Maria says.

" It's not cowboy food," Mother says.

" Is too," Maria says.

" You stupid girl," Marc says.

" You just wanna eat stew because of the picture of Rin Tin Tin on the can," Maria says.

" I do not," Marc says.

" You do too," Maria says.

" Behave yourself," Mother says to Maria.

" Shut up!" Maria says to Mother.

" Maria!" Mother says, " Jesus would never say that. Jesus would never tell his mother to shut up. If Jesus was here he would eat his supper."

" If Jesus was here,"Maria says, " I'd kill him!"

" Maria!" Mother gasps, her virgin-blue eyes bulging from her head. " What did you say, Maria?"

" I said I'd kill him, " Maria repeated.

" You don't mean that," Mother says.

" Yes, I do."

" Jesus can hear you!" Mother says in a very high voice. " I want you to say I'm sorry."

" No," Maria says.

It is Saturday afternoon and the day is ruined, interrupted by this mascarade. Maria walks past the

caragana and lilac hedges. She is dressed in her yellow
dress as though it is Sunday. She has her prayer book
marked at the examination of conscience. Only old
people and extra bad children go to confession on
Saturday afternoons. Maria hopes that Mrs. Dominiki
is not there to see her. Walking up the wide stairway to
the front doors of the church, Maria wants to turn and
run but her legs move her on. In the varnished pew
waiting for her turn in the confessional, she thinks of
telling Father Sullivan something else. Finally in the
confessional the words come out, very slowly,

     " I said I wanted to kill Jesus,"

     " Why did you say that?" Father Sullivan
asks in a deep, dusty voice.

     " Because I didn't want to eat any stew."

     " Do you want to kill Jesus?"

     " No."

     " Say Three Hail Marys and one Our Father."

     The screen divider slides shut. Maria's turn is
over.

EVERLASTING LIFE

Caterina Edwards

And now, on the edge of death, Augusta had not changed her way.

"I want another pillow,farther up," she commanded.

"There...is that the way you want it, Mamma?"

"No. I want it still farther up. I told you."

"There?"

"Pull me up a bit more."

The heavy flesh was a hanging, shapeless mass. Aurora had the feeling that if she pulled too hard it would come away in purplish handfulls from the bones. The mother she had known survived only in remnants. Her hair still dark and thick. And her eyes enormous and black. But now those eyes had become like two screens, reflecting the outside, revealing nothing from within.

Aurora settled again into the chair beside her mother's bed and into staring at the wall opposite her, blank except for a turgidly-coloured picture of Christ, smiling sorrowfully and holding his bleeding heart in hand. Anything, even that monstrosity, was better than gazing down at her mother hour after hour. She had been sitting this way for five long, long days. Ever since she'd arrived in Sicily, called back after many years by her mother's illness. Five days. Seventeen left to go. The new trimester would be beginning. She couldn't be expected to stay any longer.

Not that Augusta would understand. Even when she had less need, she felt children owed their parents everything. They had argued about it when she'd over- heard Aurora say " please " to one of her sons. " A child," Augusta pronounced, " owes his parent abso- lute obedience."

" My children owe me nothing," Aurora kept insisting, " as far as owing goes." Resisting the impulse to point out that Augusta herself had stopped living with her parents at sixteen and, from then on, except for payments of conscience money, had conducted her life as if she were an orphan. Perhaps she had judged them as the rest of society did, as little more than gypsies. They, like their parents before them, had been puppeteers, traveling about Sicily with their rainbow- coloured cart. Orlando. Rinaldo. Astolfo. The Good Christian knights against the evil Moor. The battles, tests of courage and romances. Through their mario- nettes, they gave back to the people their myths.

" Have I eaten yet?"

" Yes Mamma. Ten minutes ago."

A faint flicker in those big, almost infant-like eyes. " I have eaten then."

" Yes."

What went on in Augusta's mind, day after day? Did she see the wall? Had she ever seen it in this year she'd passed in this room? Followed each crack and curve, creating patterns as Aurora had done? She loosened her mother's grasp, gently, finger by finger. She had to wipe her hands, her face of the sweat, which she did quickly, putting her hand back before her mother called for it. It was hot and close in the small, white room in spite of the height of the ceiling and the thickness of the walls. If she opened the shutters, there was a chance of a breeze. But that would also let in the din of the Vespas and cars beeping their way along. The sounds that came through the open door from the kitchen were enough. That was the main room used by Giuseppina, the woman who owned the house, her daughters, and, it seemed, an infinite number of over-weight women, identified as relatives or friends. Most of the other rooms and the entire second floor were left to the three genteel, well-off ladies who paid high-ly for Giuseppina's care.

" Aurora!" It was a frightened cry.

" Yes, Mamma. I'm here...Do you want some-thing?"

" I don't remember."

" Oh."

" I'm always confused. My poor head can't think anymore."

" No. Don't think that way. The more you convince yourself that you're confused, the more con-fused you will become. Try and think, ' My mind is clear—I can understand'."

" My mind is clear," Augusta repeated, but with wonder and doubt.

Suddenly, Aurora's mouth was full of sour

saliva and her hands were trembling. It was her mother's fault she was in the condition she was. She'd been weakened, Aurora decided, not by the various illnesses but by a relaxing of will. Ten years ago—after a minor stroke— she'd let go. " I'm tired," she had declared. " I'm not walking again." If she had fought against age, as she used to against her husband—raging, raging, again and again.

"I would have fought," Aurora said aloud.
"What did you say?"
"Nothing, Mamma."

Aurora had always viewed her determination to continue choosing, continue growing, as an inheritance of her mother's will. Even though they had always strained in opposite directions—the mother to escape from the looseness of the bohemian world of her parents into the solid, landowning class of her husband; the daughter to escape from that stable, respectable Sicilian life to a freer, yes, looser life in California.

"One must make choices responsibly, in good faith," Aurora was fond of saying (she'd done her PhD on Sartre). And one must try to discern which side is the side of life. Her parents, she'd soon understood, were not alive but clay marionettes manipulated by their anger and resentment towards each other into repeating the tragicomedy of wandering husband and disgusted wife over and over again. Aurora tried running away at fourteen and got as far as Rome, where the police caught her. At eighteen she decided to marry, but leaving home wasn't enough. Sicily was never-changing, fired into a posture of grotesque honor, and Sicily's sun was baking her. So she'd persuaded Carlo to emigrate to the new world, although

it was rare for a middle class Sicilian to do so. They'd
gone to America to be free and it was only years later
that she understood that they had brought their strings
with them. They were caught in a tragicomedy of their
own.

" Signora." One of Giuseppina's twin daughters
in her usual uniform of jeans stood at the door.

" Yes, Letizia."

The girl lowered her head and lifted her eyes
in a parody of shyness.

" My mother wants you to come."

" Certainly."

As she disentangled her hand and got up, her
mother cried out, " So, you're leaving me?"

" No, Mamma. I'll be back immediately. I must
go and speak with Giuseppina."

The kitchen was overwhelming after the quiet
of the white room. In a corner, the two twins each
stirred a different pan on the stove, each wriggling a
jeaned bottom to an American pop song blaring from
the transistor on the fridge. Across the room Signora
Miralda lay on a red canvas cot making, uncontrollably,
little sounds to herself. Giuseppina, an enormous
woman in a pink flowered dress, sat by the central,
white marble-topped table in an overstuffed, blue vel-
vet armchair, chatting loudly in Sicilian to an equally
enormous woman with a glass eye in a straight-back
chair beside her.

" Come, Signora." Giuseppina shouted at her.
" Come. Sit. Sit, please," motioning to another stuffed
chair at the end of the table.

" Thank you." Aurora stopped to greet Signora
Miralda and squeeze her trembling hand on her way to
her chair.

" Well." Giuseppina leaned towards Aurora aggressively as soon as she was settled. " I just wanted to know if you were still thinking of calling in another doctor."

" I've called him. He's coming as soon as his office hours are done."

" Don't you have faith in the one we called. We've had the full responsibility of your mother for a year now and..."

" Of course I do. It's just a second opinion never hurts, and Mamma doesn't..."

Aurora's words died away. One of the twins switched off the radio. And everyone (even Miralda—head shaking) stared at the tiny old woman in the doorway. Aurora guessed her to be the Signora Margherita she had never seen, since the lady never descended from the second floor, but whose footsteps she'd often heard over these five days, back and forth, over and over.

" Signora Margherita," Giuseppina managed finally. " Is anything wrong?"

The lady made her way to the center of the room leaning on a carved walking stick, the back of her black robe trailing behind her.

When she reached the table, she dropped the stick and manoeuvred herself into position, one hand on the table, the other palm outward, pressed to her forehead so that her long full sleeve curtained her face. " Is anything wrong? When has anything ever been right!" Her voice was surprisingly gentle and young. She did not alter her Eleanor Duse pose. " In this life, full of filth and pain..." Aurora ran her tongue hard over her teeth to keep down a sudden fit of laughter.

Margherita dropped her arm. " What is right when
we spend our time submerged beneath putridness and the
blood of our fellow man?" Her glassy blue eyes focused
into two clear pin-pricks of light. She pointed a short,
delicately wrinkled finger at Aurora. " Life, you must
understand, is not worthy of being lived."

Everyone else nodded in tragic agreement.

" But is there something you want?" Giuseppina
insisted.

Margherita lowered herself into the chair one of
the twins had placed behind her. " I told you yesterday.
Usually the funerals pass by Via Liberta and I can see
them from my window. But the one today is a much
more important one. I forget the man's name.

" Inteso. Don Mario Inteso," Giuseppina offered.

" Whatever." Margherita's hand fluttered through
the air. " So it's been decided that the procession will
pass through Via Garibaldi. So I decided to watch from
the door."

" Don Mario was a man of honour." Giuseppina
rolled her eyes heavenward in the required fashion. " He
did all he could for my Vito. If it hadn't been for those
bastards—may all their children spit on their graves—
Vito would be here with us right now. Don Mario tried.
He tried. In the old days it wouldn't have been like this.
Those magistrates would have listened to Don Mario. "
Aurora concentrated on keeping her face blank. " My
Vito would have been with us now. A father to his daughters who need him. Need him like the bread they eat—
especially now when they reach the age when they need
prot..." Giuseppina continued, but Aurora stopped listening. She had heard the proud story of Vito the saint
before. She'd been away from Sicily too long to accept
that a man who'd kidnapped a rich young girl from Milan

and collected a hefty ransom before he was caught could be " a good man ." Perhaps Giuseppina saw him as " good " because he managed to keep part of the ransom, transforming it into expensive embroidered sheets for his daughters' dowries, a new bathroom for the house, and three hundred and eighty-five sheep.

Three hundred and eighty-five sheep. Aurora's lungs contracted. She lit a cigarette to keep herself breathing. She could see and feel slices of her dream last night. A stone road wound up a green hill. At the top of the hill stood a ruined Greek temple of golden stones. Though she walked and walked, she got no farther up the hill. Abruptly the temple disappeared. A phalanx of sheep was running down the hillside toward her. They were upon her. They butted her with their long, black snouts. They threw themselves upon her, pinning her arms and legs. She could not see. Her mouth was forced open to accept the greasy wool. She was choking.

Across the table, the friend was staring at her, the good eye neutral, the darker glass one glaring.

" Signora."

Giuseppina had stopped reciting her tale. " Please. Would you like something—some more coffee?"

" Yes." Aurora rose. " Could you bring it to the room please?"

" And some food? You ate no lunch."

" No. Thank you. As I told you before, I never eat very much."

" A soft-boiled egg?"

" No. Thank you."

" Some chocolates?"

" No. Really." This was getting to be a distorted replay of scenes, many years ago, between herself and her mother. At least Giuseppina was not likely to lock her in her room.

Aurora edged towards the door.

" Aren't you going to watch the funeral pass? It should be here any moment now." Signora Margherita half rose out of her chair. " There's going to be over thirty cars, all covered in flowers, purple and white, of course, and a hundred official chanting mourners."

" No. I think not. I better close this door too. In case the wailing bothers my mother."

" If you wait only two minutes, they'll be here."

" Two minutes!" a shriek from one of the twins. " I'm supposed to go to Maria's. I've got to get going before..." Her charge across the room, through the front door, was blocked when she passed the table by her mother, whose massive hand clamped down around her right arm.

" What do you think you're doing?"

" She has a new Dylan record...And she asked a few friends over to hear it. Will you let go of my arm? Everyone's going."

" Not quite everyone," commented the other twin, still at the stove.

" I know Maria and her harebrained parents. When you say ' everyone ' you mean there'll be boys there."

" Sooo..."

" So! What would your father say? So, what will people say if you start consorting with that so-called modern group. Stupid hussies. You have to be careful— both of you—even more than a normal girl."

" What would people say?" The phrase had been an answer to everything from why Aurora couldn't

study medicine to why she couldn't be allowed to make
her own bed. She felt a surge of yearning for her anonymous California city where she did not even know the
names of her closest neighbours.

" Mamma!"

"No!"

Both Giuseppina and her daughter were shouting
now. Signora Margherita stopped on her laborious way
to the door, turning to Aurora. She had an expression
of perfect rationality on her face and in her voice. "Cut
the balls off all the males and shove corks up all the
females. It's the solution to everything."

"But Signora," it came out in her best seminar-
leader voice,"wouldn't that lead to the end of man-
kind?"

" What do you think I've been trying to tell
you?"

The exchange fueled Aurora's smile all the way
back to the doorway of her mother's room. There the
sight of Augusta, all brown and yellow and disjointed,
on the white bed, in the white room, tensed her face
back into its habitual concerned expression. The bed
was so narrow and the room so empty and her mother
so solitary, lying there like a forgotten toy. And when,
sensing a presence, Augusta turned her face to the doorway, her eyes were intelligent with fear.

" Mamma."

"Ahhh...Aurora." Vacancy clouded over the
fear. Whom had she expected with such trepidation?
Surely Giuseppina wouldn't deserve such a reaction?
Or had there been subtle mistreatments Aurora hadn't
yet discovered?

" Why are you standing there like that? Come
here."

"Just a minute, Mamma. There is one more thing I must ask Giuseppina about."

She insisted on speaking to Giuseppina in the hall where the Signoras, the daughters and the friend couldn't overhear. "I know you told me that she never asks where he is or what happened. But does she ever mention him, ever allude to him at all?"

" No. Like I said. She chatters about you and your brother, even about Signorina Santa, her sister-in-law. But not a word about Don Vittorio. Like he never lived."

Aurora dropped wearily into the chair by the bed, returning her hand to her mother's grasp. Was it Don Vittorio's return that she'd feared? Had she pretended or had she really forgotten the man she'd slept beside for fifty years? Pretended so as to obscure the relief she felt at finally being free of him?

The bitterness between them, that was at least as long as Aurora had memory, had not dissipated in old age. When they had come to live with her in California, they had continued their tragicomedy: her father hobbling after the black cleaning woman, one hand offering candies, the other positioning itself for a feel; her mother railing, her voice a hysterical croak.

Augusta's head jerked down suddenly, waking her from her doze. "Ay..." Her eyes, this time, were panicked and vague. "Ayhhh..."

"Are you in more pain? Would you like another pill? There, you should be better soon. Lean back. It's better."

"You're a good girl, Aurora. A saint...a saint." Augusta drifted back to sleep.

Saint. Another name to the list she'd used for her willful daughter over the years. The others had been equally inaccurate but more difficult to accept. Espe- cially in the time before she had married Carlo. Even a request to be allowed to be alone with him for one hour, one week before the wedding had brought forth a tor- rent of abuse. She hadn't understood the reaction, ex- treme even for a Sicilian mother, just as she hadn't ever understood the greater mystery of how the link between two people, such as her parents, had come about. Not until a seemingly senile mutter, so unrelated to the con- versation at the time that she'd nearly ignored it, il- luminated both areas of incomprehension. " Your brother was late. He wasn't premature at all." A passion had burned for a short time between Augusta and Don Vittorio, a passion that could have dishonored the puppeteer's daughter, as many less determined reci- pients of the Don's love had been and were to be dis- honored. And she feared either alternative: ruin or marriage, for her daughter. In the end, Don Vittorio had been uncharacteristically firm and insisted Aurora be allowed her car ride with Carlo.

He had always been a gentle and generous man; Aurora felt indignation at her mother's forgetfulness. Indignation yet kinship. When Carlo had finally gone— after weeks of trying to make him understand that she wanted nó more of marriage, after weeks of finding herself answering exhortations and tears with decla- mations about freedom, truth and responsibility to self, like some George Sand heroine—her whole body had loosened. She'd rediscovered the ability to move without jerks, to turn her head without a sudden block.

" A saint. A saint." Augusta spoke in her sleep.

But she still wasn't free enough. Although they had a nurse to care for them, her mother called for her constantly. "Where are you going? When will you be

home? Why are you always going to work? Why don't
you stay with us?" Don Vittorio would check on her,
dragging his slow body down the stairs in the middle of
the night, only to walk into her bedroom and say, " So,
you are here." Or, thinking he had successfully hid himself behind the giant plant in the hall, he'd poke his
head around a leaf and gaze sorrowfully at her while she
tried to entertain a male friend.

She finally informed her brother that he had to
do something. " I need to be alone. I can't continue this
way. It's your turn."

" I can't have them in my house," he answered
as expected. " You remember how horrible it was for
poor Anita last time. It's really impossible. Still, I could
put them in a nursing home here." But Aurora balked
at the thought of Don Vittorio and Augusta, habituated
to deference and years of an aristocratic life, speaking
no English, in a nursing home in Tulsa, Oklahoma.

So, in his Christmas break, her oldest son had
taken them back to Sicily and after some inquiry, settled them at Giuseppina's. And she began to breathe
in the new silence, breathe in the empty house, free of
presences. It was so good to return at the end of a
tiring day, to find no one waiting for her, no one demanding that she begin their day. Still, sometimes the
emptiness was inside her too. And, though her thera-
pist said it was normal and would pass, it had grown
since her father died. " I made the right choice. I had
to go on living," she told her mother, still sleeping with
her mouth open and saliva trickling down a purple
crease.

" To go on living is not always the right choice
in this stinking world." Signora Margherita was standing
in the doorway. " I knocked but you didn't hear and I

thought, being such a kind lady, you wouldn't mind my..."

"Imagine. Of course not. Would you like a chair?"

Signora Margherita shook her little head. "No." She leaned forward on her stick. " I've been sitting all this time watching the funeral procession. It was exquisite." Aurora glanced nervously back. Unfortunately, Augusta had wakened and hauled herself up to a listening position. " Each car was decked with enormous garlands of purple, white and green flowers, and the hearse..."

" Please..." Aurora motioned towards her mother, who was sinking, more yellow-faced than usual, back into the pillows. " Don't speak of these things, here."

" I came to discuss another matter with you," Signora's eyes were glassy and young. " I have heard that you have a supply of pills."

" Pills?"

" To make you sleep. You take one every evening."

" Giuseppina has good eyes."

" Yes, well, no doubt as I have heard about you, you have heard my history— the tragedy of my life with my brute of a husband."

"I've heard."

" And the filthy disease he inflicted on me?"

" I've heard that you believe that."

" You understand that I long for death and that it has only been my own cowardice— I've always detested pain — that has stopped me. To swallow some pills, fall asleep and never to wake. It seems so clean, so tidy."

" Do you think Giuseppina could allow it to happen? Imagine what people would say. It would reflect on her and her house. If you took the pills, she'd only have you rushed off to the hospital. They stick tubes into you and pump out your stomach. Most painful and unpleasant."

" Well said, Signora." It was Giuseppina herself at the door, wiping the sweat from her broad forehead with her apron. " Your aunt is just driving up in a taxi."

Zia Santa had not changed much in the years since Aurora had last seen her, or, for that matter, in the years since Aurora's childhood. She was more dried out, had fewer teeth and walked bent over so that her chin was not much higher than her waist, but she was the same tiny, apple-husk doll. After many kisses and ritual greetings, both to Aurora and Augusta, she settled in a comfortable chair Giuseppina had brought from the kitchen. " I've desired to see you for many days but with this terrible flu in the air I thought it best to stay in."

" That was wise."

" One can't be too careful at my age." Santa had always been careful, cleaning everything, including the plates, with rubbing alcohol. Her apartment had always been asphyxiating. " Look at your poor mother." Santa leaned forward and whispered close to Aurora's ear. " She's close to the end, isn't she?" They both turned their faces to gaze down at Augusta who stared blankly back at them.

" The doctor thinks the situation is quite serious but we can hope," Aurora whispered back.

" And pray to our Father in heaven." The words sprayed out between Santa's remaining five teeth onto Aurora's cheek. " But she does look terrible."

" She seemed to relapse after Signora Margherita from upstairs came in and started talking of funerals."

" Oh, that one. Touched, she is." Santa leaned back and clasped the large silver crucifix hanging from her neck, as if to ward off the evil eye.

" So . How do you find me, Zia? Changed? Older?"

Santa switched her hand from her crucifix to her heavy black skirt.

" It's hard to say what you're like now, seeing you dressed like a man. You always were a contrary one. Had to do things your way. I remember you holding your breath until you turned blue once, all because your mother was trying to get you to eat a bit of chicken. From what I hear, you haven't changed much in that."

" Women wear slacks here too."

" The devil's conquering the entire world."

" What's she saying?" Augusta asked Aurora.

" She's speaking of the devil, Mamma."

" Always the same," Augusta told the ceiling.

Giuseppina's glass-eyed friend entered with a plate of cakes.

" I wondered when they were going to arrive. I made a special trip to the baker on Via Manzoni. He makes the best cream puffs in town."

" I want one," from Augusta.

The woman stayed, leaning her bulk against the window shutters and watching Aurora feed her mother. " I have a book," she said suddenly, just as Santa opened her mouth to speak, " a book that is a witness to truth."

" Do you know how to read?" Santa was annoyed.

"What do you take me for?" The woman pulled herself up and took position in the centre of the room.

" What is the truth?" Aurora kept her voice polite.

" If each one of us accepts Jesus Christ as our personal saviour, we will never die."

" By all the saints in heaven," Santa nodded at the picture of Christ just behind the woman's head and crossed herself, " by the Sacred Heart of Jesus, are you preaching to me, of all people? Do you have any idea of how many hours a day I spend on my knees?"

" Each one of us, as I did, must give up all idolatry, all false images. Each one of us must repudiate the whore of Rome." The woman's eye gleamed with fervor.

" The whore of Rome?" Santa rolled her eyes at Aurora, who thrust her tongue against her teeth.

" We must be reborn."

" Wasn't once enough?" Santa shoved her sharp chin out.

" You don't understand. I was born again. I was baptized in Lake Ontario."

" You don't need to go to some God-forsaken lake to be baptized. You can get it done at San Pietro's at the corner."

" Three hundred of us, submerged and surfacing to everlasting life."

" Three hundred of you. Must have been a big lake. Were you all naked?"

" In bathing suits." The woman was indignant.

" Well, praise the Lord for that at least."

Aurora could not hold herself any longer; the laughter burst out.

" What is it?" Her mother pulled at her hand."

" Too much," was all Aurora could manage to say, tears streaming down her cheeks.

" She's laughing at me Signora. A poor Christian woman, trying to bring eternal life to those clinging to the death of sin."

" Not at all," Aurora managed to gasp. " It's just my aunt..."

Santa smiled a gooey smile between bites of pasty. " Don't be offended, poor Christian. A pastry?"

The woman shook her head sadly on her way to the door. " You are not among the chosen."

" We're Sicilians, like everyone else," was Santa's reply to the departing back.

Augusta gasped, then let out a sudden rattling wheeze. Aurora turned back quickly to her, the laughter freeezing in her throat. But her mother was smiling back at her. She was actually chuckling. " Another sweet?"

Santa pulled her chair closer to the bed. " Saint Anthony, doesn't she look better?"

" She does." There was even a trace of fresh colour in her face.

" Knowing her, she may not have given up her will yet."

" No." Her mother was still smiling between bites.

" What are you going to do with her?"

" Before I came, I thought she was well-cared for."

" And now..."

" Well, what with the kidnapped sheep and all. I don't think it's quite...I don't like it."

" Taking her back to America?"

" I don't know." But, as she felt herself tightening, she did.

THE PROCESS

Elvina Boyko

I thought I would start with the facts. Fact: I had a grandmother. Fact: she had sixteen children. Fact: she married when she was fifteen or sixteen. Didn't like housework, worked outdoors, walking around the yard in overalls striped tan and navy. Like the ticking on the pillow I buried my six-year-old face in when I realized Grandfather was dead. Overalls with hammers and nails in the front pockets. But where did the hammers and nails float up from and how did they flow on to the paper without hesitation? Carpentry tools in her pockets. They were there in the shadows; they could easily have been fact. She walked around the yard in overalls with hammers and nails in the front pockets.

Now, where to begin? " She was a detached person," I write. " I was thirteen and homely." Grandmother probably told one of her children, probably an aunt of mine, " You'd think Sarah (she blamed my mother) could get her kid's mop of hair cut decent;

why does she let that kid wear blue with that sallow complexion; if only Sarah's kid would watch those clumsy feet of hers, she stepped into the pail of strawberries twice when we were out picking." Well, it is possible she said that. She criticized her own children, saying that , oh, I can't remember exactly, I think it was something like saying meaningfully about her son, " Yes, of course he needs money, anyone who mismanaged his farm that terribly would need money pretty bad."

So, what about my grandmother? Eileen was her favourite. Youngest of my aunts. Eileen tied old rubber rings together into a rope (we watched in admiration) and showed us how to skip, she let us help her bake cookies, she sneaked the gallon of wine upstairs for us one Christmas. Eileen danced her weekends away, always threw her clothes in heaps on the beds, never sewed on buttons. She drank like a fish, her older sisters said disapprovingly. (" What do they know?" I thought). And she liked Johan.

Pause in another reality. I eat, I sleep, I read. I read: " Defining yourself with your mother's approval". " Time flips a coin and our mothers become our children." There is my mother, always there is my mother." I sleep, I think. Yes, of course—conscious mind— this will be a short story about a mother-daughter relationship. I do not even wince as I set down the words in my notebook, " I will write a mother-daughter relationship."

" Grandmother was a detached woman, she criticized her adult children as if they were strangers, I was not pretty, I was not her favourite grandchild." Why was she detached? Well, she had sixteen children (one died in infancy). She was, then (sixty-three at her death minus forty-three for my mother who was second oldest at the time of her mother's death) eighteen when the first child...forty-one at the time of Eileen's... Which—fact— is an average of one child every one decimal four years. She was, then, nearly always pregnant for twenty-three years of her life! Suddenly an image, Grandmother, her stomach swollen..." She bends down to pick up some old boards; she is cleaning up behind one of the granaries. She has trouble bending over, the grass is pale, sickly-yellow under the board and she feels slightly nauseated, puts her hand to her belly and suddenly the universe reels within her head. She cannot remember which child this is, feels like she is on a treadmill, machine of flesh, child after child wearing the gears in her head, she cannot for a wild instant remember how many children she has had, or if she has had any. Then the sun hits her closed eyelids, she remembers she has to get some potatoes peeled for dinner for someone, she can't remember who, and the dozen loaves of bread are ready for the oven, and she has to get the cream from the icehouse. She straightens, walks towards the house, dazed. Four or five children come dashing, screaming towards her, " He hit me, no he hit me first, tell him to stop it, no this is what really happened.." And the woman firmly pushes them away from her big belly, says, " Go away, go away and play for a while, just leave me alone for a little..."

So that is why she is detached! She wants to remain sane, she must remove herself one step to keep from being smothered by fifteen personalities descending upon her all at once.

I am humbled by what I have just learned about her, awed by the thoughts that go around her, in her head, as she bends over the yellowing grass, ants scur-

rying out from around the pale blades. Some wick in
me touching deep, deep, some vague collective inheritance, the fluid drawn up slowly as I am artificing.

Part two. Grandmother and Eileen. She let
Eileen grow up on her own, she didn't discipline Eileen,
Eileen did what she wanted. Did they ever try to talk to
one another? When I was fifteen I needed someone to
talk to. I walked around the lake through the drying
yellow grass, thought of suicide, cried myself to sleep
every night. One night I couldn't control my weeping,
burst out into wailing like some war orphan. My mother
rushed in, stood detached, in the shadows. Finally her
voice, "What have you to cry about? I've got more to
cry about than you and do you ever see me crying?"
Eileen is sobbing and my grandmother says, " Do you
ever see me crying? Eileen is crying about Johan who is
going to marry Elsa who Grandmother says is a blonde."

Now Eileen has to become Ellen so that Johan
can say to her, " My Ellen of Troy." " He puts his hand
against the back of her neck the way she likes it, tosses
her hair, tells her fondly that she is a foolish child, his
Ellen of Troy. He is thirty and she is sixteen and mad
about him. But she detaches herself, laughs, will not be
betrayed or made a fool of by this feeling she has never
encountered before. In her home it is a point of pride
not to show affection. She laughs, even though she is
shattering inside, when he sits brooding in the dark car
where they have parked by the town cemetery. He sits
staring blankly and then bursts out bitterly, ' But how
can I leave? The oldest son. The old man is depending
on me to take over the business.' She feels near some
abyss, the danger takes her breath away, she does not
know how to deal with the flood of some feeling which
is roaring about her; love is absurd, she thinks des-

perately. And, her heart pounding, begins to tease,
" Come on, I know of a better business, come on,
smile.' And he realizes he is not alone in the car, finally
tossles her hair, says, trying to smile, ' You're such a
sweet foolish child.' Into her hair, ' That's what I adore
about you.' "

" One day Grandmother tries to talk to Eileen
about Johan." One day my mother is altering a dress.
Her fingers are warm on me, brushing my skin, pressing
along my arm and shoulder, her breath sweet on my
cheek, I can reach out and touch her face if I want to.
She says, " I don't know why you're so careless about
clothes, you could see it wouldn't fit," and yet she
isn't concerned about the style I chose, allows me to
decide on my own. " I'll just take the seam in here..."
her mouth full of pins, " this dart...then the hem of
course..." and she is suddenly happy. She always is
when she's working, just like Grandmother who loves
to be milking cows, pitching bales, repairing fences. I
stand hypnotized under my mother's hands, wanting
her touch, hating it, I can't move under her spell.

" With her fingers touching her daughter's
flesh through the fabric, my grandmother says to
Eileen, ' I hear old man Melnychuk bought his son a
house—Johan, isn't it?—he's not planning to get married, have you heard? Saw him in church with some
blonde, tall, skinny, she doesn't smile much. They say
she's six years older than him.' And Eileen says,'Oh,for
God's sake, how should I know? Can't you finish this
dress already, can't you hurry up and finish it?' And
Maria the mother hums under her breath, her expression inscrutable, her breath warm on her daughter's
face."

Maria? But my grandmother's name was Marie.

Yet she must be Maria. Because, fact: this woman I am
making feels softer, fuller, more deep than the thin
flat sound of "Marie".

Part one. "Maria comes to visit Ellen, her daughter, in the city. Ellen is thirty. Maria is an old woman,
thin, pale, shuffling a bit." My great-grandmother
Anastasia shuffled around in her homemade mocassins,
wouldn't wear dentures, and had the most beautifully
wrinkled skin I had ever seen. I was eighteen and she
was eighty-seven and we were good, good friends and
talked together in Ukrainian. And she liked me as Maria
had never. And Anastasia was gentle and humble. Maria
needs more softness, some gentleness, so I'll give her
some of Anastasia's mellowness.

"Ellen says, 'Here's my report card,' tosses it
on the table. Maria takes off her gloves, she's been re-
storing furniture abandoned in the granaries and in the
old summer kitchen ("Western Poverty", Ellen's brother
Nicholas calls the style). Maria glances at the Failed to
Pass. She glances at me, puts on her gloves. 'So?' she
says carefully. ' I'm quitting,' I say. She picks up the
sanding board, begins sanding down the table again.
'Well,' she says. 'Well, who am I to try stop you?'
Furious, I say, 'Well, I don't care. And I'm not going
to tell Father. You tell him.' (I ask Johan slyly,'Who's
Elsa?' His face turns white, he grips my arm, 'Listen,
you mind your own business. You're full of life and I
see more of you than I should. But you're young. And
you're spoiled. You don't know about a woman like
Elsa.' The world is tumbling around my ears. I draw
myself together, laugh in his face, ' You're so moral
it hurts.')

"Now I look at the old woman Maria, sitting
across the room from me, sipping tea, her left hand

motionless (a shed has fallen on her as she helped her
sons move it, crushing her left...). I remember saying to
my friend Judy, ' That's one thing about my old lady,
she'll never pry. I can leave opened letters on my desk
and I know she'll never look inside. She never snoops
around.' Now I say, ' Remember Mom, how you'd
never search our rooms or our pockets?' Maria looks
up, the edges of the dark irises blurred as if the brown
is running into the whites of her eyes (my God, she
can't even see that well any more). ' Why should I have?
I had enough work of my own, without looking for
more trying to clean up your rooms.' I can't tell if she
is misunderstanding deliberately. Then, Judy had rolled
her eyes, ' You lucky shit. My old lady has to know
every little corner of my mind, she's always snooping
around.' Judy, whose brother was Johan." Call him
Adam. Except that he was not the first. Ellen's
initiation will come much later and not with Johan.
Call him Jean. " Thick sandy hair, eyes that pale blue
they always are when he is intoxicated, which is every
weekend when he is free from the family business. I
walk up boldly, say, ' Hi, you're Judy's brother, aren't
you? Wanna dance?' Unmoving, he is rooted to the
earth, unmoved by my hand on his arm. He says
roughly, ' I don't dance, come on, let's get out of
here,' his hand an iron grip on my arm." Earthy and he
must remain so and he must be one of her own race.
(She later meets, let me see...Sean who is Irish and in
the Army and then Sun Lin the artist). Johan. Rooted.
Earth sign Taurus. And the name in her language—
Taras. " It was Taras she could have loved if she had had
the courage."

     I eat. I sleep. I visit my mother in a reality which
is not the same reality as the one my story exists in. I

ask her questions it has never occurred to me to ask before. " How did you feel once all six of us had left
home? How did you manage with the first three of us
being exactly a year apart? How did you meet Father?
What kind of child was I?" I revise my story. My mother
and I are changing and the story has to be changed.
Re-vision. Maria and I speak with softer voices now, we
look at one another with a difference. And yet, I cannot
control some things: " I say to Maria, ' Remember how
Victoria always wanted to be a doctor?' Maria sniffs,
' A lot of good her fancy ideas did her. I told her she'd
only be a nurse.' Controlling my fury— mother what
flows in your veins? — I think, the best o.r. nurse they
have, they all say it whatever hospital she ends up in,
Victoria who still wishes she had...'Well, you could have
encouraged her.' Maria looks up sharply, ' Am I to take
the blame for all of my children's mistakes? What am
I? God?' "

Part three. " My mother is old, I feel my own
flesh greying (they say once we pass fifteen our cells
stop replacing themselves. I have been dying for fifteen years now. We both drive one another's flesh
greyer). If only____were coming home now instead of
tomorrow, her young body bursting through the doorway, her eyes burning with energy, my gut burning,
wondering what my mother will think of my daughter."

And so it is I discover I have a child. Born un-
expectedly in the middle of a phrase, she fits herself
into the story and now the story, what came before the
child, what comes after, is altered, expands, and must
further expand. The story begins to be mother and child
and the child's child, patterns, breaking of patterns, love,
inability to love, youth, age, rhythm, dissonance, a-
symmetry, death, life. Intricate threads weaving them-

selves in and out of the story. For a child is born, chris-
tened Mary, then Mary-Ellen, then Marilyn, a blend of
Maria-Ellen. And yet the sound retaining its own iden-
tity, not synonymous with either, not opposite, not
supplementary or complementary. An intricate, organic,
asymmetrical blend.

The separate elements, heated, have blended,
heat precipitating some marvellous alchemical process
by which the elements blend, never again to be recog-
nizable. Never again the separate original elements of
the other reality. Life, like a mirror, has shattered me
into a million pieces and I give back now the myriad
reflections.

BIOGRAPHICAL NOTES

ELVINA BOYKO grew up on a farm near Tadmore, Saskatchewan. She presently lives in St. Albert, Alberta. One of her stories, "Tapestry" was published in *Interface 1*, 1976.

TERESE BRASEN was born in St. Boniface, Manitoba, but has been an Edmontonian most of her life. She is now living in Bragg Creek, Alberta, while working on a novel. "Princess" is her first publication.

CANDAS JANE DORSEY was born in Edmonton; she lives on a farm near Calmar, Alberta, and works as a child-care worker in Edmonton. She has published three books of poetry: *this is for you (1973)*, *Orion Rising (1974)* and *Results of the Ring Toss (1976)*, all with blewointmentpress, Vancouver. She has also published a story in *Branching Out*.

CATERINA EDWARDS was born in Wellingford, England and came to Alberta at the age of seven. She now lives in Edmonton and teaches Canadian literature at Grant MacEwan Community College. Her stories have appeared in *Journal of Canadian Fiction* and *Branching Out*.

MYRNA KOSTASH was born and raised in Edmonton and is a widely published free-lance journalist. Her features have appeared in *Saturday Night* and *Maclean's*, and she is now writing a book about the community of Two Hills, Alberta, and its particular Ukrainian-Canadian ethnicity. She has had two stories published in *Descant*.

HELEN J. ROSTA lives in Edmonton. Her stories have appeared in *Fiddlehead*, *Prism International*, *Quarry*, *Journal of Canadian Fiction*.

ARITHA VAN HERK was born in Wetaskiwin, Alberta and grew up on a farm near Edberg. She is a graduate student in English at the University of Alberta and is now working on a novel. Her poems have appeared in *White Pelican* and a story by her won the *Miss Chatelaine* short story contest for 1976.